THE CHALLENGE OF IMMIGRATION

Vic Cox

—Multicultural Issues—

ENSLOW PUBLISHERS, INC.

44 Fadem Road   P.O. Box 38

Box 699   Aldershot

Springfield, N.J. 07081   Hants GU12 6BP

U.S.A.   U.K.

To Inge, Sabrina and my parents,
for their contributions, past, present, and future.

Library of Congress Cataloging-in-Publication Data

Cox, Victor I., 1942-
  The challenge of immigration / Victor Cox.
    p. cm. — (Multicultural issues)
  Includes bibliographical references and index.
  ISBN 0-89490-628-3
    1. Immigrants—Government policy—United States—Juvenile
literature. 2. United States—Emigration and immigration—
Government policy—Juvenile literature. I. Title. II. Series: Multicultural issues
(Springfield, N.J.)
JV6483.C66 1995
325.73—dc20   94-34645
                                                      CIP
                                                       AC
Printed in the United States of America

10 9 8 7 6 5 4 3 2

Illustration Credits: Vic Cox, pp. 19, 64; Linda Garrett/*El Rescate*, pp. 16, 72;
Library of Congress, pp. 33, 35; National Archives, pp. 26, 30, 44; Joaquin
Romero/*El Rescate*, p. 49; U.S. Immigration and Naturalization Service, pp. 8, 11,
29, 38, 45, 47, 61, 63, 92, 96, 98, 100, 103; Charley Van Pelt, p. 107.

Cover Photo: Susan Hopson.

Contents

The Battle Over Immigration

In 1993, Juvenal Garcia celebrated his first July 4th as an American citizen. His wife, Lucia, and their two children, and Garcia's mother, father, and some of his ten brothers and sisters and their families all went to a beach near Santa Barbara, California, for a holiday picnic with bittersweet overtones. In becoming a naturalized American, Garcia had to renounce his Mexican citizenship. "I'm happy and proud to be an American," he said. "But it's kind of hard. My heart is still in Mexico."[1]

It took Garcia twenty-two years to forge his decision. Then he tried taking the citizenship tests in English twice before he passed them.

Garcia, who has fought a stutter since childhood, took special classes and was helped by his eleven-year-old daughter, Blanca. Now he has his citizenship papers.

On that same American holiday Garcia was celebrating, the U.S. Coast Guard intercepted off Mexico's Baja California a trawler packed with illegal immigrants from China. Liu Jiang, a twenty-two-year-old teacher from Fujian province, was on board. Because he was trying to make converts to Christianity, Liu told United States authorities, villagers and officials in China harassed him for a year before forcing him to flee. Of the 658 United States-bound Chinese on three boats rounded up that week off Mexico, only Liu won a hearing for political asylum. It made worthwhile the $10,000 smuggler's fee and the three months of hunger, filth, and cramped quarters he had endured.

When Mexico returned the rest of the boat people to China, Liu flew to an Immigration and Naturalization Service (INS) detention center in southern California. While awaiting a full hearing on his claim of religious persecution, he told a reporter, "I really feel that coming to America is just like going to heaven."[2]

Desperation and hope have always propelled people from their homelands in search of a better life. Their destinations are not usually developed regions like North America or Western Europe. It takes money to get to these countries, and some kind of support system to be able to stay there. The United Nations Population Fund reported in 1993 that most of today's annual flow of approximately 100 million international migrants move from a poorer to a richer developing nation. Thirty-seven million fled from wars and natural disasters.[3] Distinctions between refugees and economic migrants are blurring, the fund's report noted, because political turmoil and economic collapse often go hand in hand.

The massive migrations of the past two centuries have had large areas of thinly populated land to settle, like the Americas or Australia. From 1820, when immigrants first began to be counted systematically, through 1992, the United States alone accepted nearly 60 million newcomers.[4] Many such former escape valves are now sealed, or in the process of being sealed, while population pressures mount.

The Immigration Debate

A rising tide of newcomers, and their concentration in a few states, has renewed debate over immigration's value to America. Fueled by economic recession, flaws in past reforms, and growing concern over illegal immigrants (noncitizens who break laws to live here), many people and politicians are urging sweeping changes in the way America regulates immigration. A 1993 *Newsweek* national opinion survey asked if immigration was good or bad for the country today: 60 percent of the respondents said bad and 29 percent said good.[5] In a California poll taken the same year, 17 percent of respondents said cheap labor was the prime benefit of foreign immigration, while another 17 percent said cultural diversity; 43 percent saw no benefits to the country at all.[6]

When the questions turned to illegals, the sentiments became harsher. To 86 percent of the Californians, illegal immigration was a moderate to major problem. They ranked it below only the economy and crime among the state's problems. This feeling is also reflected in Congress where some lawmakers support a constitutional amendment to deny citizenship to anyone born on United States soil whose parents were here illegally. (Currently, children born on American territory are automatically American citizens, whatever the nationality of their parents.)

Those who believe that immigrants were crucial to building the United States into the world's primary democracy and economic power argue that we cannot turn our backs on refugees and new immigrants. People fleeing persecution and seeking a better life for themselves and their families are our heritage and our future. They work, pay taxes, create jobs,

This thirteen-year-old Latino boy was strapped underneath a car in a vain attempt to smuggle him into the United States. Illegal immigration is a major concern to the United States and other nations.

and contribute to the community. We must keep open the golden door for our long-term national gain as well as for humanitarian concerns over people's safety and well-being, is the viewpoint of this side of the debate.

That was then and this is now, counter their opponents. The United States doesn't have free land for homesteaders anymore; we have overpopulated, polluted cities where immigrants converge, adding to urban problems and taking jobs from the native-born. Our public school and health care systems are disintegrating under a tide of non-English-speaking users. Welfare and law enforcement systems are also burdened by poor, violence-prone immigrants, especially illegal ones flooding across our southern border. We cannot afford to be so generous any longer, they conclude.

Newcomers in the 1990s

Both sides of the debate agree that immigrant numbers are soaring and that the historical pattern of where they come from has changed. United States government figures show that annual legal immigration jumped from nearly 600,000 in 1982 to 1.8 million in 1991, for a total of 8.6 million in ten years. Close to the historic high point of 10 million immigrants who entered the United States between 1905 and 1914, the numbers are actually inflated by 2.5 million former illegals who came in from the cold during this period under a one-time amnesty.[7]

Also lessening the impact of newcomers was a much larger population than in earlier years. The average annual rate from

1905 to 1914 was 11.1 immigrants per 1,000 United States residents, while the 1982 to 1991 ratio was 3.5 per 1,000 residents.[8]

In fact, in the high-watermark year of 1991, fewer than four out of ten people who became legal permanent residents were recently arrived immigrants. The remainder had been living in the United States for years, which was one of the qualifications for amnesty.

While those who have been legalized, as well as current illegals, are important to the debate, they are minor players in comparison to the number of legal immigrants. More than 70 percent of the newcomers since 1982 have arrived and set up residence through various legal channels that are described in Chapter 3.

Who are the legal immigrants of the 1990s and from where do they come? INS data offers limited information on the newcomers. From 1941 to 1990, four out of five of all immigrants were under forty years old and 55 percent were female.[9] Occupations were diverse, with only 6.5 percent reporting agricultural jobs between 1976 and 1990, while 25.5 percent had work as unskilled or semiskilled laborers, 23 percent as professionals or managers, and 20 percent were in domestic service.

Of the 704,000 nonamnestied immigrants admitted in 1991, the seven most commonly represented nationalities were, in descending order: ex-Soviet Union (57,000); Philippines (55,000); Vietnam (55,000); Mexico (53,000); mainland China (32,000); India (31,000); and the Dominican Republic

Country origin of legal (nonamnesty) immigrants in 1991

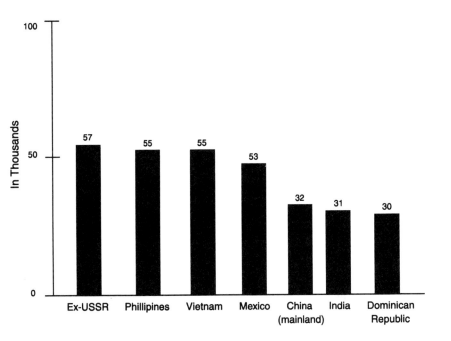

Based on figures from Immigration and Naturalization Service

(30,000).[10] These figures underline the current dominance of Latin Americans and Asians in the immigrant flow. Since 1955, Europeans have accounted for 20 percent of legal United States immigrants, Asians and Pacific Islanders for 30 percent, while 48 percent were from the Americas (including Canada).[11]

Where the Immigrants Live

During the 1970s and 1980s, major cities across the nation felt the growing presence of Latinos and Asians. Newcomers tended to settle in established immigrant communities where many spoke their native language; they might know or meet people from their home regions and hear about work possibilities. Such advantages concentrated immigrants in a few states, principally California, Texas, New York, Florida, Illinois, and New Jersey.

These six states took in three-quarters of the legal 1991 immigrants; they also have been the leading states for newcomers' intended residence each year since 1971.[12] California has been the top choice annually since 1976. From 1989 to 1991, the state absorbed nearly 1.9 million (42 percent) of all immigrants, including the amnestied. Texas and New York each took in around half a million (11.5 percent) during this period.[13]

The Los Angeles–Long Beach metropolitan district was 1991's preferred destination. New York City came in second. Chicago, Illinois; Miami–Dade County, Florida; and the California areas of Anaheim–Santa Ana and San Diego drew roughly equal numbers of legal immigrants. A closer look reveals that of the fifteen United States metropolitan districts with the heaviest immigrant influx, eight were in California, two in Texas, and one each in New York, Chicago, Miami–Dade County, Washington, D.C., and Boston–Salem, Massachusetts.

Together, these areas housed better than half of the year's total 1.8 million legal immigrants. School districts, hospitals, and public health services struggled to meet the increasing needs of impacted cities and neighborhoods.

Illegals and the Amnesty Program

Adding to the complexity of the debate over immigration is a substantial population of illegal residents, whose impacts, real and imagined, have stirred much emotion. With the Immigration Reform and Control Act of 1986 (IRCA), Congress tried to solve the problem by punishing employers who knowingly hired illegals. At the same time, an amnesty program was set up to legalize those people who had been living unlawfully in the United States before 1982.

By most accounts, the amnesty has so far produced more results than employer sanctions. The amnestied amounted to 1.1 million, or 61 percent, of 1991's total immigrants. Four out of five came from Mexico. The majority of the remaining legalized population came from Haiti, El Salvador, Guatemala, India, and Pakistan.

The rise of illegal populations, particularly in California, Texas, and New York, and their challenge to border control, raise serious issues for Americans. But a complex body of rules govern legal immigration, and the people who go through this process should not be confused with those who don't.

"We must separate apples and oranges," says former United States immigration official Harold W. Ezell. "Legal immigration is good and illegal immigration is bad."[14] Not everyone agrees with such stark judgments, but distinguishing between legal and illegal immigrants is necessary whenever the data make it possible to do so.

Even language has become part of the debate. Terms used to discuss immigrants and their problems have come under attack. The word "alien," which is used in United States immigration laws as well as press reports to describe noncitizens, has a sinister ring to many. "We prefer the term 'undocumented worker' instead of 'illegal alien.' It makes people sound as if they're from outer space, or something," explained Oscar Andrade, executive director of a Central American aid group in Los Angeles known in Spanish as *El Rescate* (The Rescue).

While agreeing that language can be a barrier to clear thinking as well as to communication between people, others warn that words should be substituted with caution. Author and think-tank researcher Joel Kotkin noted, "By insisting on the word *undocumented* instead of *illegal*, the advocates seem to be challenging the validity of United States law itself."[15]

Mixed Feelings on Immigration

Americans have long held differing opinions about legal immigrants. They take pride in the nation and the way of life forged by their predecessors, but feel uneasy about letting others in to continue the process. Mixed feelings toward newcomers frame many debate questions, among them: Do immigrants take jobs from American citizens or expand the economy by consumption of goods and services? Are legal, or illegal, immigrants taking undue advantage of welfare? Does the spread of Spanish threaten English as America's standard language? Can the mainstream absorb the mostly Latino and Asian newcomers and remain unchanged, or is a new, multicultural society in the making? What can be done to secure United States borders against the smuggling of illegals?

This book explores these and other questions, but there are very few clear-cut answers. Truth may be found in differing views, though the pros and cons of immigration are more complex than opponents usually acknowledge. And events often have a way of pushing reason to the sidelines.

Anti-immigration advocates' fears were reinforced in early 1993 when legal immigrants were accused in violent criminal acts in Virginia and New York. In January, a sniper killed two Central Intelligence Agency employees and wounded three others outside the CIA headquarters' main gate near McLean, Virginia. The prime suspect, whose request for political asylum was still being processed, fled to his Pakistan homeland. Authorities there cooperated with the United States in seeking him.

Even more lethal was the February van-bombing of New York's World Trade Center, which killed six people and injured more than one thousand others. Subsequently, the

FBI said it had broken a terrorist conspiracy to bomb the United Nations, several other sites in Manhattan, and to assassinate United States and world leaders. Grand jury indictments linked fifteen suspected plotters to the World Trade Center bombing and named Sheik Omar Abdul Rahman, a blind Muslim cleric, as their leader. All legally entered the country, and two are citizens.

This wave of criminal activity coincided with incidents of smuggling ships packed with Chinese nationals running aground in northern and southern California and New York

The rising number of refugees from Asia and the Americas in the 1980s sparked conflict over their treatment by government agencies. This protest took place in front of the Los Angeles City Hall.

City. Altogether, the U.S. Coast Guard estimated that around two thousand illegal Chinese boat people were caught in the first seven months of 1993, compared to only twenty in 1991.[16]

The Advocates

The passion surrounding immigration issues has created assorted national political organizations that are leading the public debate on the subject. Their positions range from a complete ban on immigration to opening the borders to all newcomers, and they all have figures to back their arguments.

Caution is advisable when evaluating numbers used in regard to immigration. When British statesman Benjamin Disraeli observed that there are "liars, damned liars, and statistics," he could have been commenting about the figures that have been gathered on illegals. The situation is not much better for legal immigrants.

A National Research Council panel studied the data and collection methods used by eleven United States bureaus, including the INS, the main agency for admitting, processing, and deporting immigrants, and for turning them into new citizens. The NRC panel's 1985 report concluded: "The INS and other government agencies produce masses of data, if not always timely and not always accurate, about immigrants, refugees, and the foreign-born, but the data are not what we need to answer the fundamental policy issues of the day."[17] This book relies on the best available government and private sources, but cannot vouch for figures cited in advocates' arguments.

Among the most visible advocates of increased restrictions

on all immigration is the Federation for American Immigration Reform (FAIR). Founded in 1979, FAIR's literature describes itself as a Washington, D.C.-based "public interest organization [that] seeks to improve border security, to stop illegal immigration and reduce legal immigration through a moratorium." It claims 50,000 members nationwide, and has branches in the cities of Sacramento, San Diego, and Los Angeles, California. The federation believes that "today more immigrants are entering this country legally and illegally than at any time in our history," and that this is against the best interests of the people, economy, and ecology of the United States.[18]

Dan Stein, executive director for FAIR, regularly testifies before Congress and provides an anti-immigrant viewpoint to the media. In 1992, he urged House lawmakers to hire more Border Patrol agents, build barrier walls along key sectors of the southern border, consider a mandatory, fraud-proof work permit and driver's license for citizens and noncitizens alike, and to convert abandoned U.S. military bases to "detention centers for criminal . . . and other aliens."[19] FAIR seeks to limit total immigration to around 300,000 a year, but has proposed suspending admission of most immigrants indefinitely.

Often facing off against FAIR is the National Immigration Forum, a coalition of about 150 immigrant and civil rights organizations, trade union, church, and legal groups. Led by Executive Director Frank Sharry, the Washington, D.C.-based coalition is dedicated to "defending and extending the rights of refugees and immigrants in the United States." The National Forum, formerly known as the National Immigration,

¡SALVADOREÑO!

Si tenes el TPS, es sumamente importante que apliques para el nuevo programa del DED en el cual existe la posibilidad de su extensión. El programa del DED te sigue protegiendo contra la deportación y te da un permiso de trabajo.

Además, tenes el derecho de aplicar para el asilo político bajo los beneficios de ABC y te dará protección para más tiempo a vos y a tu familia.

El plazo para aplicar para el DED se vence en junio, 1993.

VENGA A REGISTRARSE AHORA EN CARECEN o EL RESCATE

¡NO ESPERE HASTA EL ULTIMO MOMENTO!

PARA INFORMACIÓN DEL DED Y ABC LLAME O PRESENTESE A

CARECEN
660 S. Bonnie Brae
Los Angeles, CA 90057
(213) 483-6800

EL RESCATE
1340 S. Bonnie Brae
Los Angeles, CA 90006
(213) 387-3284

A privately-published Spanish language poster advises refugees from El Salvador on changes in United States political asylum rules and urges registration before the program's deadline. Many nonprofit immigrant aid groups play vital roles in government outreach efforts.

Refugee & Citizenship Forum, "came together in the 1980s specifically to fight the tide of xenophobia sweeping across the country," according to its literature.[20]

Sharry also lobbies Congress and says his coalition's victories include: the admittance of "reasonable numbers" of refugees and immigrants; the recent amnesty program that had legalized more than 3 million illegals by 1992; and court-improved rights and opportunities for Salvadoran and Guatemalan refugees. The National Forum advocates legal immigration of around 800,000 annually and opposes any moratorium. But it also supports improved border controls to cut illegal immigration.

"We agree [with FAIR] that as a sovereign nation, the United States has a right and a duty to control our borders," said Sharry. "We disagree over means."[21] He added that eight out of ten immigrants are legally in the United States and that racism plays a role in the move to exclude people, particularly in feeding fears generated by the World Trade Center bombing.

"If we start focussing on a few crazies who commit heinous crimes, we're going to lose sight . . . that it's in our interest to bring families together, to bring in workers who create economic growth, and to rescue a few refugees who are standing up for what they believe in," he said. "I hope America will remember that our country is based on people who weren't wanted [elsewhere]."[22]

2

A History of Uncertain Welcome

Immigration was a potent political issue well before the official birth of the United States. Wars with France and Spain extended England's New World domain south to Florida and east to the Mississippi River. The crown needed more settlers to farm the lands won in the treaty of 1763, and to replenish its war-depleted treasury with new taxes. Yet Britain chose this moment to clamp down on America's immigrant pipeline.

Some scholars think a shift in the migrant flow from English to Irish and German settlers prompted Britain's actions. From thirteen families, who arrived in Philadelphia in 1683, the number of German immigrants and their descendants rose to an estimated 100,000 by the eve of the Revolution.[1] In any case, among the reasons for separation cited in the 1776 Declaration of Independence were the crown's restrictions on migration to America and refusal to grant English citizenship to people of the thirteen colonies.[2]

Fourteen years after that famed Declaration, the first federal Congress set standards for naturalized citizens. The 1790 Naturalization Act restricted citizenship to a "free white person" who had lived at least two years in the United States.[3] Over the next decade, naturalization law changes stretched the residency standard up to fourteen years, then back to five, as political factions battled in Congress to control the immigrant vote.

Noncitizens were directly affected by a package of 1798 laws that historians lump together as the Alien and Sedition Acts. Under these laws, the president could order deportation or wholesale imprisonment for immigrants deemed dangerous to the peace and safety of the country. The naturalization part of the package required a fourteen-year residency period, banned "enemy" nationals from citizenship, and kept the color bar.[4] Only with the Fourteenth Amendment to the Constitution in 1868 did former slaves and their descendants gain naturalization rights. For Asians, race blocked this path to citizenship until well into the twentieth century.

Anti-immigrant hostility, known as nativism, was not confined to nonwhite nationalities or ethnic groups. It infected some of America's founders. Benjamin Franklin criticized German immigrants for being clannish, ignorant, and preferring their own tongue to English.[5] He groused that the Pennsylvania State Assembly would need interpreters because elected representatives lacked knowledge of the English language.

One objection to German immigrants, which persisted long after Franklin, was that they were largely Roman Catholics in a predominantly Protestant population. Catholicism was the religion of most Irish settlers, too, though the Scotch-Irish were Presbyterians. By 1817, more Irish and Germans than Britons were debarking at America's seaports. The United States admitted 143,000 immigrants between 1820 and 1830. Over the next twenty years at least another 2.3 million arrived; nearly 70 percent were Irish and German.[6] This sixteen-fold increase in newcomers came during a period of inexpensive sea transportation and frequent United States economic crises.

As steamships replaced sailing vessels for well-to-do passengers, travel time from Europe to America dropped from months to weeks. To stay in business, sailing ships cut prices to capture the immigrant market. Settlers in the 1850s could get from English or Irish ports to America for as little as $10 a head. Immigrants had to provision themselves for the forty- to sixty-day voyage, could not count on adequate drinking water, suffered in unventilated, cramped quarters, and feared an outbreak of disease that might end in death. An estimated 10 to 20 percent of those who embarked did not survive the Atlantic crossing.[7]

Nativism's Ebb and Flow

In the 1830s, anti-immigrant sentiment combined with anti-Catholicism to create a strong nativist political movement. The nativists argued that America's republican form of government could not last if many citizens owed allegiance to the pope. They looked down their noses at people they considered superstitious, uneducated, and a threat to jobs held by the native-born. In 1834, a mob burned a convent school in Charlestown, Massachusetts.

Nativists gained support because immigrants would work for less money than established jobholders, and were often hired to replace striking workers. While some employers used the threat of hiring immigrants to keep their work forces in line, others found it to their advantage to play to antiforeign feelings by advertising jobs with the warning, "No Irish Need Apply."

In 1844, the nativist American Republican Party elected six congressmen and dozens of local officials in New York, Boston, and Philadelphia.[8] In the years before the Civil War, nativists formed secret societies to agitate against Catholics and for limits on immigration, which was then regulated by each state.

Another nativist political group, the Order of the Star-Spangled Banner, was better known as the "Know-Nothing Party," because its members were pledged to secrecy. At their peak of power in 1854, the Know-Nothings had seventy-five seats in Congress and six state governorships.[9] Their strength coincided with the decade in which nearly 1.5 million Irish Catholics struggled to America when potato crop failures spread famine and death throughout Ireland. In the 1840s and 1850s, foreign-born settlers made up 10 to 11 percent of the total population.[10]

The Civil War displaced nativism from America's political scene, and the Know-Nothing Party vanished. But anti-immigrant prejudices and ill will were just below the surface. Times and scapegoats might change but the fear of foreigners did not. More often than not, it surfaced under pressure of war or economic stresses such as depressions, and targeted the most vulnerable racial and ethnic groups.

Asians and the Color Bar

The Chinese farmers, who dribbled into California in the 1840s to pan gold and work the mines, eventually immigrated in substantial numbers. The Civil War's end unleashed a rapid rail expansion to the West and in territories wrenched from Mexico. With an eye on a cheap source of labor, the rail barons supported an 1868 treaty with China that allowed unrestricted immigration of its people.[11] Famines in the province of Canton added push to the pull of railroad, mining, and agricultural jobs, and nearly 200,000 Chinese immigrants entered between 1861 and 1880.[12] It was the first large-scale movement of Asians to the Americas.

It did not last long. Fueled by economic booms followed by busts, and fanned by nativist groups, fear and hatred stalked Asians. Californians, who had charged Chinese immigrants a head tax to come into the state, in 1879 denied employment to the same people by a constitutional amendment.[13]

Anticipating this statewide initiative was an 1876 report on Chinese immigration from the California Legislature that was openly hateful of the Chinese. It said, in part: "During their entire settlement in California they have never adapted themselves to our habits, mode of dress, or our educational system, have never learned the sanctity of an oath, never desired to become citizens, or to perform the duties of citizenship, never discovered the differences between right and wrong, never ceased the worship of their idol gods, or advanced a step beyond the traditions of their native hive . . ."[14]

In 1882, Congress overrode a presidential veto and voted to deny U.S. citizenship to foreign-born Chinese and to ban migrant laborers. The Chinese Exclusion Act stayed on the books until 1943 and was also used against other Asian

Angel Island in San Francisco Bay was the major West Coast processing station for Asian immigrants in the late nineteenth and early twentieth centuries. A disembarking group wears a mix of traditional dress and modern fashions.

nationalities. Immigration from Asian nations stayed low until the 1970s.

Like the first Chinese, the initial Japanese who came to the United States were migrant laborers, including some students, who hoped to make their fortune and return home. Between 1885 and 1907, some 157,000 Japanese contract workers—many sponsored by the government in Tokyo—came to till Hawaii's sugar-cane fields.[15] Thousands of these men went on to California where the ban against Chinese workers left openings for the Japanese, many of whom settled down and sent for waiting wives or so-called picture brides.

Racial tension erupted in 1906 when the San Francisco school board ordered that Japanese children must be taught in segregated classes. The Japanese government objected and President Theodore Roosevelt, labeling the act "a wicked absurdity,"[16] persuaded the board to reverse its ruling. Nevertheless, within two years Washington and Tokyo agreed to a number of measures that ended Japanese labor migration to the continental United States. An important but divided core population remained—the Issei, Japanese who were legal residents but barred from citizenship and the ballot box because of their race, and their American-born children, the Nisei, who were automatically citizens.

For years, the Issei struggled against state and federal laws chaining them to inferior economic and political status. They challenged anti-Asian laws in the states of California and Washington that prohibited them from owning or using agricultural lands. But on reaching the United States Supreme

Court they lost every case. The high court likewise ruled against Issei requests for naturalization, holding that they were covered by the Chinese Exclusion Act. In 1924, Congress reaffirmed the color bar by denying immigration to all Japanese. As citizens, the Nisei grew up with the right to own agricultural land and vote. Then came war with Japan in 1941 and, the next year, the forced internment of 120,000 Issei and Nisei men, women, and children, nearly two-thirds of whom were citizens.[17] By presidential directive and congressional action Issei and Nisei alike were forced from their West Coast homes and businesses to live in isolated concentration camps under military guard for an indefinite time. Justified as a wartime safety measure, the massive uprooting of so many citizens was unprecedented in United States history, and comparable only to forcing Native Americans onto tribal reservations.

In 1988, Congress and the president issued a formal apology to Americans of Japanese descent for their World War II detention. A fund was set up to pay $20,000 to each of the concentration camps' approximately 78,000 survivors.[18]

Riding Immigrant Waves

As the chart shows, immigrants have come to the United States in four distinct but unequal periods since about 1820: the old system of open immigration between 1821 and 1882; a new, federally restricted immigration from 1881 to 1929; a national quota era between 1929 to 1968; and the present

Immigrants Admitted: 1820—1991

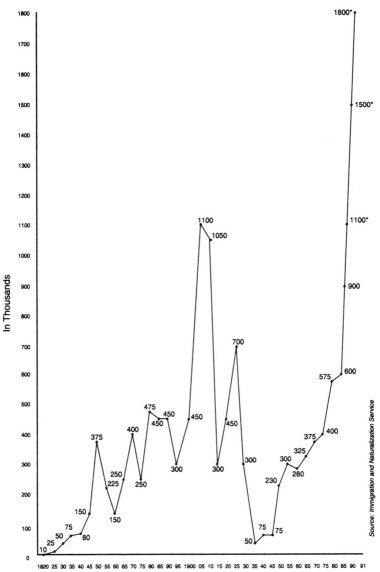

Source: Immigration and Naturalization Service

* Includes amnestied applicants

1989–500,000   1990–900,000   1991–1,100,000

period based on family reunification, job skills, amnesty, and restriction of illegals.

Though individual states set some immigration standards, during most of the period until 1882 immigration was generally unrestricted. Around 10.2 million people arrived between 1820, when data began to be collected regularly, and 1880. These participants in what social historians like to call the "old immigration" came chiefly from northern and western Europe.

From New York's Ellis Island, a little boy points to a mist-wrapped Statue of Liberty, a gift from the French people to America. The federal government took control of all immigration in 1882 and barred entry to Chinese laborers that same year.

Congress made 1882 a watershed year by suspending imported labor from China, and federalizing control and responsibility over all immigration. Initially, Washington had to contract for processing and inspection services from the states. Besides New York harbor, which had Castle Garden receiving station, other major ports of entry included the cities of Portland, Maine; Boston, Massachusetts; Philadelphia, Pennsylvania; Baltimore, Maryland; Key West, Florida; New Orleans, Louisiana; Galveston, Texas; and San Francisco, California.

Criminals and prostitutes had been listed as "inadmissible" immigrants as early as 1875. To these restrictions Congress added others, barring entry to "lunatics, idiots," or anyone likely to be a "public charge," that is, to require public assistance. The first federal immigration fee, a head tax of fifty cents, was imposed on each émigré coming by water.[19]

It took the federal government years to build the present structure of coastal and border controls. In fact, immigrants in cabin class on ships and those crossing over from Canada and Mexico were not regularly counted until the first decade of the twentieth century.[20] The head tax was levied to discourage the poorest immigrants. It rose to $8 a person by 1917 and stayed there until it was abolished in 1952.[21]

From 1881 to 1930, around 27.5 million immigrants entered the country legally through United States ports.[22] During these years, the annual flows came from the mostly agricultural nations of southern and eastern Europe, principally Austria, Bulgaria, Greece, Hungary, Italy, Poland, Portugal, Romania, Russia, Spain, and Turkey.

More than 11 million were from Italy, Austria–Hungary, and Russia alone. They fled poverty and in many cases persecution, particularly Russian Jews who were the target of frequent campaigns in their homelands, called pogroms, designed to force them to emigrate for fear of their lives. The newcomers brought customs, clothing, languages, and religious practices that seemed strange to those who had preceded them. They looked and acted differently, and soon suffered for it.

In one example, after the murder of the police chief of New Orleans, eleven Sicilian immigrants, including three Italian citizens, were arrested and locked up. On March 14, 1891, a mob stormed the New Orleans jail and hanged all of the suspects. The resulting diplomatic crisis with Italy was settled when the Italian government accepted a $25,000 indemnity for the victims' families.[23]

A Changing America

America had also changed from a farming to an industrial society. By 1890, the cheap land of the frontier was gone; new arrivals looked for jobs in the expanding cities. Some brought skills that were needed in the mills and factories; many did not. The unskilled concentrated in city slums and survived on piecework and peddling wares, hauling trash, and servicing their better-off neighbors. Actor Kirk Douglas's father, who collected rags for a living after fleeing Russia, was one of them. Fully one-third of the immigrants in the last two decades of the nineteenth century took jobs as unskilled laborers.[24]

The twentieth century began with the highest number of newcomers America had ever seen. More than 10 million landed in the United States between 1905 and 1914, and three-quarters of them were processed through New York. Great steamships carried newcomers across the Atlantic in ten to twelve days, a pace that challenged even the huge receiving station on Ellis Island in New York harbor. Originally opened in 1892 with a capacity for 10,000 émigrés daily, the facility and the island itself expanded over the next two decades to handle this vast movement of people. In the peak year of

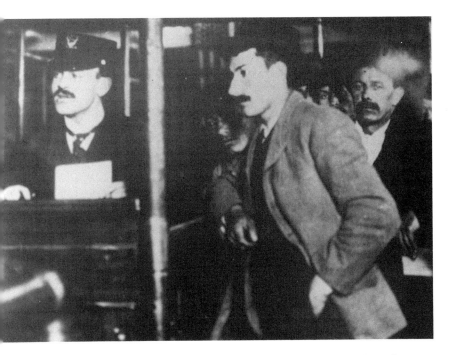

Italian men are questioned by one of Ellis Island's inspectors in the early days of the twentieth century. More than 1 million immigrants were processed this way in 1907, the peak year for the station.

33

1907, slightly more than one million immigrants landed at Ellis Island; another quarter million were processed through other U.S. ports.[25]

Even before the number of foreign-born reached 15 percent of the total population in the 1910 census, the highest proportion it has ever been, the clamor for more restrictions was rising. Government inspectors already turned back people who they judged medically unacceptable or likely to become charity cases, or who fell into groups that Congress barred from entry, such as criminals, anarchists, contract laborers, or various Asian nationals. But no more than 2 percent of a year's total number of immigrants were actually deported.[26] This was not enough to satisfy reborn nativist groups such as the Boston-based Immigration Restriction League, or those who advanced the league's agenda.

Congress passed English literacy requirements for immigrants three times between 1894 and 1915, and the president vetoed them every time. On the fourth try, in 1917, Congress overrode Woodrow Wilson's veto and added literacy to the entry qualifications. This law also prohibited the immigration of natives of a geographic zone that included all of India, parts of China, and most other Asian and Pacific island nations.

After World War I, which forced a drop in émigrés, America turned inward again. This time there were not only restrictions on who could come, but also on how many immigrants were allowed in. The National Origins Act of 1924 set quotas—numerical limits—on people coming from specific countries. It reduced the volume of immigrants, favoring northern and western nations over the rest of Europe. For the first time, the law required foreigners to secure entry permits, called visas, in their homelands whether they planned simply to travel or to settle permanently in the United States. Latin America and Canada were not included in the original national quota system, which took full effect in 1929.

Quotas and Illegal Immigrants

Illegal immigration of Europeans who came in through Canada and Mexico was a growing problem, so the 1924 law also funded the Border Patrol. Crossing the border at any but

Ellis Island—this scene is from 1905—was the gateway to America for around 12 million immigrants over a span of sixty-two years. It had its own hospital, laundry, bakery, kitchen, transportation, and money exchange facilities.

specific ports of entry had been outlawed since the 1890s, but enforcement was sporadic and inadequate. National quotas unintentionally created "a great rise" in illegal immigration, according to *An Immigrant Nation,* the official INS history of immigration regulation.

By the 1930s, the government's emphasis had shifted from admitting people to excluding and deporting them. From 1931 to 1970, some 7.4 million settlers took up permanent residency, 1.4 million fewer than had arrived between 1901 and 1910. During the quota-enforced low immigration decades, outside events still influenced who was allowed in.

The worldwide Great Depression and World War II generally limited applicants, though around 250,000 refugees from Nazi persecution managed to find loopholes and unfilled quotas that allowed them in. Once the war against Germany and Japan ended, sympathy for refugees and war brides enabled thousands more to enter. The Cold War also shaped the United States immigrant flow as Congress and the president repeatedly fiddled with restrictions in the name of internal security, approving influxes of Hungarian escapees or Cuban exiles. From the passing of the Displaced Persons Act of 1948, through 1960, nearly 800,000 refugees and asylum-seekers found shelter under various humanitarian programs.[27]

Though wartime pressures forced the repeal of the Chinese Exclusion Act in 1943, labor shortages led Congress to import temporary agricultural workers, primarily from Mexico, that same year. Economic and political interests backed renewal of this temporary measure, which put migrant workers in orchards and fields throughout the nation, until public pressure ended it in 1964.

Abolishing Nationality and Race Quotas

The following year, national quotas were replaced by a visa system of first-come, first-served, with priority given to reunification of families and to immigrants with needed skills. Race and ancestry as well as national origin were abolished as immigration criteria. Civil rights leaders hailed the changes.

Entries from North, Central, and South America were limited to 120,000 for the first time, while the rest of the world was allotted 170,000 visas. However, immediate relatives (spouses, minor children) of United States citizens and certain other special immigrants, such as ex-government employees, were exempt from the ceiling. These exemptions were extended under the Refugee Act of 1980.

Weakened by recessions in the 1970s and 1980s, the United States system shuddered under the impact of refugee families fleeing Asia and Central America and the dramatic growth in illegal immigration. Between 1970 and 1991, almost 13.7 million immigrants were given permanent residency. However, nearly one-third were either refugees or former illegals already in the country who became legalized through the amnesty program of the late 1980s. The 1.7 million refugees accepted over this twenty-one-year span represented about two-thirds of all refugees admitted since World War II ended.[28]

More dramatic than the numbers was the shift from

Annual legal immigration

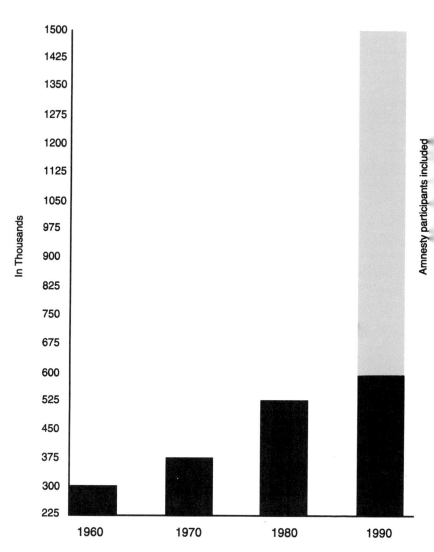

Based on figures from Immigration and Naturalization Service

European to Latin American and Asian immigrants. Until the 1960s, Europeans accounted for at least half the settlers in any decade. With the 1965 amendments, newcomers from the Americas and Asia became the majority, reversing a two hundred-year-old pattern. Between 1970 and 1991, 85 percent of all legal immigrants came from these regions.

Mexicans dominated the legal Latin immigration with 2.3 million newcomers during the last two decades, followed by the Dominicans, Cubans, Jamaicans, and Salvadorans. Canada contributed around 350,000 immigrants, which placed it between Jamaica and El Salvador in numbers. From Asia, nearly 973,000 people entered from the Philippines, with lesser numbers from, in order, Korea, China, Vietnam, and India.

A 1990 overhaul of immigration laws loosened restrictions and raised the worldwide limit to 675,000 visas a year. Combined with the 1986 amnesty program, these policies added many new legal residents to the population. What disturbs today's citizens and lawmakers is that the number of present and incoming illegal residents is neither known nor effectively controlled.

chapter

3

The World of Immigration Laws

Immigrants' contributions to this country are recognized when it is said that the United States is a nation of immigrants. But exceptions are hidden by the truth of this generalization. Overlooked are the ancestors of Native Americans, who greeted the English settlers when they first landed in what is now called New England.

Some American citizens of Mexican heritage who today live in Texas, New Mexico, Arizona, Nevada, Utah, and California have family roots that date back before the present states existed. These western states were carved from lands taken by force from Mexico during the U.S.-Mexican War of 1846–1848, or were subsequently bought in the Gadsden Purchase of 1853.

The single largest ethnic group forcibly incorporated into America were Africans sold into slavery. Between 1619 and 1808, when Congress banned the trade, countless thousands of unwilling black men and women were shipped to America as slave labor, mostly for the South's rice- and tobacco-growing regions. When the Civil War broke out in 1861, the slave population numbered nearly 4 million people.[1]

With these historical exceptions, the bulk of the United States's current population is composed of people, and their descendants, who *chose* to live in this country. They emigrated from all over the world, some fleeing war or famine, religious or political persecution; some to find economic and personal security. Whatever the reasons behind the individual choices, they wanted a better life for themselves and their children than was possible in their homelands. America was the key to their dreams.

Turning Dreams into Reality

Those dreams endure in today's immigrants and refugees, but turning them into reality has become more difficult as the nation's population grows and its economy changes. For more than a century, the United States has placed restrictions on newcomers, deciding who and how many may come in, and has tried to foster business and tourism without losing control of its borders. These often conflicting goals are the basis for immigration laws that define types of entry permits or visas, set numerical limits on some kinds of visas but not on others, and do away with them in certain cases.

For example, the Immigration Act of 1990 set aside a total of 36,000 immigrant visas for certain categories of employees of large United States businesses in Hong Kong for the years 1991 to 1993. Visas for displaced Tibetans, on the other hand, were held to a total of 1,000 for the same period. In another special program during this time span, no entry permit was required for nationals of twenty-one selected countries, mostly in western Europe, who came to the United States on temporary business or for a vacation.

Some programs and special quotas aim at handling specific problems, such as the backlog of would-be immigrants. The State Department reported 2.4 million registered applicants awaited immigrant visas in early 1990.[2] An even larger problem is the load on border inspectors who checked an estimated 455 million citizen and noncitizen entries at border crossings, airports and seaports around the nation in 1991. Many of these entries were people who live in Canada or Mexico and cross the border daily for work or shopping.

Types of Visas

Except for the limited visa-waiver program and the workers who daily cross over from Mexico and Canada, most people enter the United States legally through three main avenues: with an immigrant visa, a refugee visa, or a nonimmigrant visa. The first two visa categories require the immigrants or refugees to have American sponsors and allow them temporary or permanent residence on United States soil. Though the law treats refugees and immigrants differently, the aim is to set them on the road to citizenship. Their sponsors guarantee that they will have a place to stay and that they will not require public assistance for at least the first three years.

Nonimmigrant visas are for short-term visitors such as tourists, businesspeople, government employees of other nations, and students. Sponsors are not required for such visitors, nor is citizenship permitted with this type of visa. But it is possible to enter as a nonimmigrant and later change status to that of permanent resident, a necessary step for anyone hoping to become a naturalized citizen.

The 1990 law raised United States immigrant visas to a worldwide total of 675,000 annually, as of October 1994. (For transition purposes, an extra 25,000 visas were issued annually during the preceding three years.) The visas were to be distributed in this way: 71 percent were for family members of legal residents, 21 percent for job-skill-based immigrants, and 8 percent for people from thirty-six nations negatively affected by previous immigration laws.[3] This last category helped European countries like Ireland and Poland, which had seen their visa quotas drop under post-1965 admittance formulas. Refugee visas are separate from the worldwide total, and are issued under a formula that changes somewhat each year.

Congress has created a complex and shifting world with laws that separate people into various kinds of immigrants. Despite attempts to balance national quotas with personal and family factors, new backlogs of visa applicants have been created by solutions to old logjams. Top priorities go to the reunification of families, to those with needed skills, and to refugees; other special groups, such as clergy, rank lower.

Within these categories, some relations are preferred over

others, and not always for obvious reasons. For instance, a citizen's unmarried sons and daughters, and their children (if any), will get visas to immigrate before any married offspring and their families.[4] These family preference visas fall under the numerical quotas. However, Congress decided that any citizen could bring over immediate relatives—spouses, minor children, and parents—and that they would not count against immigrant quotas. In 1991, more than 237,000 family members gained permanent residence in this way.

The Canadian/United States border also has a history of illegal immigrant crossings, as recalled by this border control stop in the 1930s. The U.S. Immigration and Naturalization Service estimates that 100,000 Canadians are living illegally in the United States, but only 1.5 percent of the total apprehensions in 1992 were made along the northern border.

The INS says that most people granted permanent residency that year were exempt from worldwide quotas. Besides immediate relatives, there were exemptions for the amnestied, for refugees and for asylees,[5] the INS term for people seeking asylum. Just under 300,000, or 17 percent of the total, were admitted under existing quotas. Granted, amnesty participants skewed the percentages in 1991, but exemptions have paved a broad path for legal immigration.

Who Obtains Visas?

Visa applicants learn that the rules are subject to United States public opinion, as well as political whims, and that they change frequently. But, in general, applicants must win permission to enter by convincing State Department and immigration officials they fit the law's definition of a desirable immigrant: the person must be of good moral character, not carry a contagious disease—in early 1993, tuberculosis,

Legal means for entering the United States

DOCUMENT	REQUIREMENTS	PERMITS
Immigrant visa	Sponsors	Eventual citizenship
Refugee visa	Sponsors	Eventual citizenship
Nonimmigrant visa (for short-term visitors)	No sponsors required	Citizenship not available

leprosy, AIDS, and five other sexually transmitted diseases could disqualify applicants—not abuse drugs, be financially self-sufficient, and be unlikely to become a burden on society. For some workers, the Labor Department must certify that jobs are available to the newcomer because employers cannot find citizens to fill them. This is the case for migrant or special agricultural workers (SAWs).

United States economic and foreign policy interests often shape the rules of the game. Ten thousand visas a year are set aside for immigrants with $1 million to invest and who will create at least ten jobs. If the investor is willing to gamble on investing in rural areas or zones of high employment, the visa's capital requirement drops to $500,000.[6] The program has not been wildly successful; only a little over 100 investors had taken this offer by early 1993.

After the Soviet Union's collapse, Congress worried about what might happen to scientists involved in nuclear weapons research. Not wanting the former Soviets to work on bombs in other countries, a 1992 law allowed 750 nuclear scientists and their families to immigrate to America over a four-year period. The ex-Soviets were allotted part of the 140,000 annual visas reserved for those with special skills or money to invest.

The Naturalization Process

All legal immigrants, including refugees, are issued temporary work and residence permits by the INS or the Labor Department. Once in the United States, most newcomers, even if they are married to citizens, must live here for three to five years before they achieve permanent resident status or start the naturalization process. At that time, the INS classifies them "permanent resident aliens," popularly known as green-cardholders because these permits used to be that color (current ones are pink and white).

In addition to the long wait before applying for naturalization, the prospective citizen must be at least eighteen years old, pass tests in English, swear an oath of allegiance to the United States—and endure standing in long lines at each stage of the process. The tests measure oral English understanding, ability

In 1963, then-Attorney General Robert Kennedy witnessed a swearing-in of new citizens in Washington, D.C. At that time, most immigrants were of European origins; now most come from Asian and Latin American nations.

to read and write in English, and knowledge of American history, structure, and philosophy of government.

More than 308,000 people were officially naturalized in 1991, and it took most of them eight years to do it.[7] About half of those new citizens came from Asian homelands, a pattern true since 1981. The largest groups in the class of '91 were from the Philippines (33,700), Vietnam (29,600), and Mexico (22,000).

Looking at one year's crop of new citizens gives a partial picture of naturalization. In fact, the INS says, "a large proportion of immigrants never become citizens."[8] The permanent resident who forgoes citizenship enjoys the same rights and protections as a citizen—except that he or she gives up the right to vote in nearly all local, state, or federal elections or to hold elected office. The INS, which does not routinely track how many legal immigrants become citizens, says their impression is that nationalities with the highest citizenship rates come from Asia (except Japan), Africa, and Eastern Europe, while the lowest rates are from Western Europe, Canada, and Mexico.

Because of a growing delay in swearing in new citizens, Congress tried to speed up the process. The oath of allegiance, which had traditionally been administered only by judges, may now be given by either an INS official or a judge, according to the immigrant's wishes.

Refugees and Asylees

Under United States law, anyone outside his or her homeland who does not want to return because of "a well-founded fear" of persecution can claim protection as a refugee or seek political asylum. (The legal difference between a refugee and an asylee is the location from which they apply: the refugee can apply from outside the United States; the asylee must be on American soil.[9])

Both refugee and asylum applicants undergo mandatory screening because they receive federal aid that is withheld from other legal immigrants. For example, the government helps certified refugees and asylees find jobs as well as resettle, it funds English classes for them, and, for the first eight

In 1990, a Central American-oriented refugee support group called *El Rescate* (The Rescue) created a temporary wall inscribed with ten thousand names of civilians who had been killed in El Salvador's civil war. Students read from the wall while it was located in Los Angeles.

months after arrival, it provides medical aid and small cash grants to particularly needy refugee families.[10] Refugees and asylees, who enter as temporary residents, also need only one year before they can change status and secure green cards.

The Haitian Dilemma

Sometimes the humanitarian aims of United States immigration policies clash head-on with political realities. Such was the case with Haitians who fled their Caribbean island after a military coup ousted the elected government in 1991. Thousands risked their lives in flimsy wooden boats on the 600 mile voyage to Miami.

During the 1991–1992 exodus, the Coast Guard intercepted about 37,000 Haitians and sent one-third to a makeshift camp on the U.S. Naval Base at Guantanamo Bay, Cuba. Here they were able to apply for asylum because they were on American territory. Though it took more than a year to finish the process, 11,000 Haitians found refuge in America. Others subsequently took their places in Guantanamo.

However, a group of 250 to 300 boat people, who were infected with the virus that causes AIDS, found themselves in legal limbo. United States officials said they qualified for political asylum but their disease barred them from entry. Some Haitians were confined, with inadequate medical care, for fourteen months or more. In June 1993, a federal judge ruled that the infected Haitians were illegally detained and had to be admitted.

Church-led resettlement programs, under the INS's Community Relations Service, distributed Haitian asylees to Massachusetts, New York, Florida, and other states. Among the last asylees was Michel Valsaint, a former agriculture extension agent, who held on to his hope and humor. "I came from Haiti, where it is bad, and I went to Guantanamo, where it was worse. Anywhere else should only be better," said the twenty-nine-year-old exile upon his arrival in Miami.[11]

The day Valsaint arrived, the United States Supreme Court ruled that the president has the power to exclude "any alien," adding that the 1980 Refugee Act did not apply outside United States territorial waters. However, the problem of asylum abuse remained untouched by these rulings.

Under current law, anyone who lands on United States soil and seeks asylum has the right to evaluation of the claim, a procedure that can take eighteen months or more. The length of time depends on the workload of the area INS asylum officers. In the meantime, there is insufficient capacity for detainment so a hearing is set and the applicant is permitted to live and work legally in the area. The INS has no means of tracking all would-be asylees, so it relies on their voluntary return for the hearing. Many simply vanish into the urban landscape.

In 1992, nearly 104,000 new asylum applications were filed. As a result of policies, inadequate resources, and court decisions, INS has a backlog estimated at around 300,000 applications, mostly from Central Americans living in the Los Angeles area.[12]

Nonimmigrant Visitors

In many ways, foreign visitors are the tail that wags the immigration hound. Some 19 million nonimmigrant admissions were recorded in 1991 by the INS. (One person may account for multiple admissions.) In fact, 78 percent of entries were for tourism, 14 percent for business, and 8 percent were divided among students, employees of foreign governments, and others.[13]

Faced with an overwhelming crush of traffic, the INS since 1988 has suspended, or waived, nonimmigrant visa requirements for citizens from twenty-one selected nations. The program is reciprocal, so American travelers get the same treatment from these mostly European states. But such expediting of nonimmigrant arrivals and departures risks that someone will overstay his or her allotted time.

Again, the INS has no way of tracking an individual's whereabouts once in the United States. This has led to abuses, with people arriving on valid visas and then taking their chances in the shadows of illegality. An INS survey of 6,200 amnestied noncitizens classified 21 percent as "visa overstayers."[14]

In addition to the visa-waiver program, border crossings by millions of Canadian and Mexican citizens for short-term business or pleasure are loosely inspected and require no visas. Canadians may travel without restrictions or visas for up to six months; Mexicans have crossing cards valid for seventy-two hours and a distance of up to twenty-five miles from the southwestern border.[15]

Border-crossers represent nine out of ten of the estimated 294 million noncitizen admissions in 1991. Citizens going in or out of the country added 160 million inspections to the total. That year, San Diego, California, and El Paso and Laredo, Texas, were the nation's three most heavily used ports of entry.

Main gateways and immigrant streams may change, but American borders have long been porous and, since national quotas were established, a persistent problem—particularly when there are more and better jobs on one side of the border than on the other.

Jobs and
the Immigrant

Street vendors daily spread their wares outside the federal building housing the INS and FBI headquarters in New York City. Most of the peddlers are immigrants, many of them illegal, and all are selling to survive. They are part of an estimated 10,000 unlicensed street vendors plying their trade in the city.[1] One T-shirt peddler from Guinea told a *New York Times* reporter, "This is better than welfare, no?"

In Chicago, legal Korean immigrants have pooled their resources to form a cooperative fund that lends money to members for small businesses. A traditional form of sharing economic risks in Korea, this co-op, or *kehs,* has brought both consumer and employment opportunities to sections of largely black south Chicago.[2]

Jefferson Boulevard in south Dallas, Texas, was a dying inner-city business district in the early 1980s. Now, nearly 800 shops and enterprises have transformed the area. About three-quarters are Latino-owned, many by immigrants who, according to community leader Leonel Ramos, "were hungry enough to start their own businesses."[3]

These snapshots of immigrant-inspired economic activity are generally positive. Nothing could be more natural to Michael Fix, an immigration issues researcher for the private, Washington, D.C.-based Urban Institute. "It's sort of a fact of life that immigrants generate growth," he said. Colleague Maria Enchautegul found that immigrants, legal or illegal, helped create more jobs in urban areas than did native entrepreneurs. She thinks part of the explanation for this difference is the energy and ambition that drive people to leave their homelands and strike out on their own.[4]

Job-Takers or Job-Makers?

There is another view, one that casts immigrants as job-takers rather than job-makers. One of the oldest and most durable arguments against legal immigration holds that it steals jobs from native-born workers, and/or lowers wages by increasing competition for existing jobs.

"Immigration is currently flooding the labor market, primarily in the low-skill, low-wage sectors, and driving down wages and working conditions for many Americans. . . . Because our immigration policies . . . [do] not take economic conditions and unemployment into account, we continue to import new workers even when many Americans are losing their jobs," contended a paper published by FAIR, the Federation for American Immigration Reform.[5]

Citing a study of Los Angeles janitorial workers, FAIR

said that immigrants displaced a largely unionized African-American work force. While total janitorial employment rose by 50 percent between 1977 and 1985, the number of union members dropped from 2,500 to 600. FAIR also said that, in 1992, the INS issued 1.3 million work permits "to legal and illegal immigrants. This exceeded the net number of new jobs that were created in 1992."

"Immigration is destroying the American middle class," concluded Dan Stein, the group's executive director.[6] However, his evidence seems contradicted by FAIR's own calculations or outdated by events. Breaking down the 1992 total of legal and illegal immigrants, FAIR came up with 170,000 less than the number of work permits they said were issued, and not all those immigrants were of working age.[7] Similarly, Los Angeles news reports place janitorial union membership at 7,000; they confirm that many new members are illegal Latin women immigrants.[8]

No Simple Answers

Lawrence Harrison, a former official of the U.S. Agency for International Development, detects negative economic forces as a result of immigration: "The availability of cheap labor skews investment decisions downward toward low-tech, low-wage, employment-intensive production."[9] Such pressures keep United States wages lower and hold back technology in comparison to other advanced countries, like Germany and Japan, Harrison argued.

On the other hand, some economists maintain that increased

immigration of people older than eighteen refreshes the United States labor supply. Immigrants represented one-quarter of all new workers between 1980 and 1988, while making up 9 percent of the total work force at the end of that period.[10] As native-born workers age and have fewer offspring, immigrants' importance will increase for at least parts of the economy.

Labor economist Thomas Muller sees mixed consequences from these pressures and changes. Immigrant workers "enhance the competitiveness of [local] industries," according to his research. Expanding payrolls multiply jobs throughout the region, for natives as well as for other immigrants. Not everyone shares equally in job growth; some occupations suffer, Muller says. For example, in manufacturing, restaurants, and retail trade, immigrants take more jobs than they create; the situation reverses in utilities, communications, and public sector jobs such as teaching and law enforcement.

Migrant Workers

Many migrant and seasonal field workers, who may number between 3 and 5 million, are legally working and living in this country. Illegal immigrants are blamed for keeping migrants' average earnings at around $5,000 a year, but other factors are also at work. For instance, Florida Rural Legal Assistance had to go to court to get growers to pay $51 million in back wages withheld from sugarcane workers, who tend to be Caribbean-born.[11] The state's roughly 200,000 migrant workers include immigrants from Jamaica,

Haiti, El Salvador, Guatemala, and Mexico as well as many African-American citizens.

Farming accounts for less than 3 percent of America's work force. That figure has stayed about the same for twenty years because, growers say, immigrant labor fills shortages created by a lack of native workers. Agriculture is held up as an example of how America benefits from immigration. Lower labor costs mean lower food prices, allowing most Americans to eat better and the nation to export surplus crops. Others say the hidden costs of this deal are workers suffering from poverty—poor housing and nutrition, diseases like tuberculosis and pesticide poisoning, undereducated children—and stunted technological progress.

Wages may be depressed or kept low by immigrant labor in low-skill sectors such as agriculture, domestic service, and garment manufacturing, some economists say. These areas, along with restaurant and hotel service, are traditional employers of immigrants. Minority native workers may be displaced in these sectors, or they may become qualified for better, more skilled jobs, but the jury is still out.

Similar effects are not found in high-skill sectors, most economists claim. Within professions like medicine, skilled immigrants usually fill gaps created by technology or specialization. For decades, shortages of native-born nurses have been met by recruiting overseas. Parts of rural America depend on immigrant physicians to supply the bulk of primary care. Half of Illinois's 12,000 immigrant doctors practice outside the cities and suburbs. The percentage is thought to be even higher in other midwestern states.

Muller noted that job-stealing by immigrants has never been substantiated for native-born workers as a whole, but that the effect has been to push natives from manufacturing and low-skilled jobs into the white-collar sector. He admitted that "the relationship between job opportunities for these workers and immigration is complex and not fully understood by economists."[12]

Myths and Confusion

The National Immigration Forum labels the whole job-stealing argument a myth. "Almost all the relevant research has found immigrants do not displace native workers," it said. "In truth . . . immigrants stimulate local economies, create jobs, and pay far more in taxes than they receive in benefits."[13] The National Forum quoted a 1990 report by the U.S. Council of Economic Advisers to the president that pointed out "numerous studies suggest that the long-run benefits of immigration greatly exceed any short-run costs. The unskilled jobs taken by immigrants in years past often complemented the skilled jobs typically filled by native-born population, increasing employment and income" for Americans as a whole.

The confusion over who gets what jobs, especially in hard economic times, is one reason the issue becomes oversimplified. A 1993 *Newsweek* national opinion poll revealed that 62 percent of those surveyed believed immigrants take jobs from native-born workers.[14] This general fear—reflected in earlier surveys—runs counter to the consensus of most economists and academic studies. These studies tend to emphasize long-term gains over short-term losses, and national benefits instead of local costs.

Those opposing the consensus cite Rice University economist Donald Huddle, who concluded that one low-skilled native-born worker was displaced for every four new immigrant workers. On this basis, Huddle estimated that immigrants bumped more than 1 million such workers from jobs in 1992, and that these displaced people cost $6.1 billion in public assistance.[15] His projections and research have been criticized, but Huddle's studies point to costs other than unemployment, issues to be taken up in the next chapter.

Skills and Education

Short-term impacts may benefit some industries and injure others, but how well immigrants do in the long run depends largely on their skills and education. A major study of future United States labor needs warned that the economy's mix of skills is "rapidly moving upscale, with most new jobs demanding more education, and higher levels of language, math, and reasoning skills."[16] Some predict this work-force trend will impact heavily upon immigrants.

Legal newcomers are split between the highly skilled and well-educated and those with minimal education and few skills. The National Forum argues that immigrants "are as well educated and skilled as their native counterparts,

Immigrants admitted by occupation group, 1976 – 1990

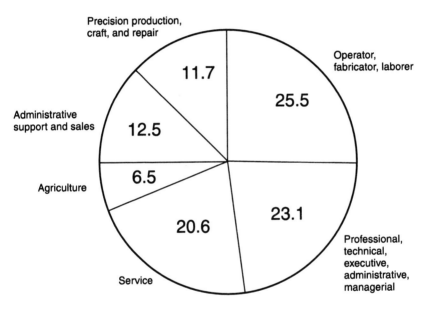

Precision production, craft, and repair — 11.7

Operator, fabricator, laborer — 25.5

Administrative support and sales — 12.5

Agriculture — 6.5

Service — 20.6

Professional, technical, executive, administrative, managerial — 23.1

Source: Immigration and Naturalization Service

perhaps even more so."[17] But the better educated turn out to be a smaller portion of the immigrant stream than the less educated. One-third of recent legal immigrant workers were high school dropouts, while one-quarter were college graduates.[18] The remainder were in between.

George Borjas, a University of California labor economist, is confident that "immigrants have little impact on the earnings and employment opportunities of natives." But he worries that the skills and earnings potential among those arriving between 1950 and 1980 is in a significant and steady decline.[19] Lower levels of education and economic development in the homelands of most Latino and Asian immigrants do not explain this, he cautioned. Part of the answer seems to be that the United States economy has created more low-paying jobs than high-paying jobs. When citizens avoid the low-skilled, low-paying jobs, these are filled by immigrants, especially illegal ones, who find them an improvement on what they can get in their native countries.

Illegals in the Workplace

Immigrant employment issues heat up over the role of illegal workers. It was not until the 1986 Immigration Reform and Control Act (IRCA) that hiring illegal noncitizens was outlawed. Closing this large loophole in immigration control was designed to turn off the job magnet for illegals. It was backed by fines against employers who flouted the law and those who turned down job-hunting legal residents and citizens because of their accent or how they looked. Enforcement, however, has been spotty.

Many illegals do not stay in the United States, though no one knows how heavy the voluntary return traffic is to Mexico and other countries. One indicator of involuntary returns is the number of expulsions, nearly 33,000 in 1991, in which noncitizens admitted illegal status and paid for their own trips home. There were some 126 nationalities in this group, and nineteen individuals had more then 100 expulsions each. Mexican nationals made up two-thirds of the expulsions.[20]

United States Immigration and Naturalization Service agents found illegals working the fields of this farm and sent them back home. Checking up on 3 to 5 million migrant workers, most of whom are in the United States legally, is a huge task for the INS.

Workplace information is equally elusive, but recent amnesty programs offer some insights. In a major 1989 survey, 94 percent of 6,200 former illegals said that economic reasons prompted their migration; 62 percent mentioned family ties.[21] Males had a slightly higher employment rate than comparable native-born workers, while females were at the same rate; however, the jobs they held were very different. Twice as many legalized workers as natives held blue-collar jobs; they were seven times more likely to be serving as household help or food-service workers.

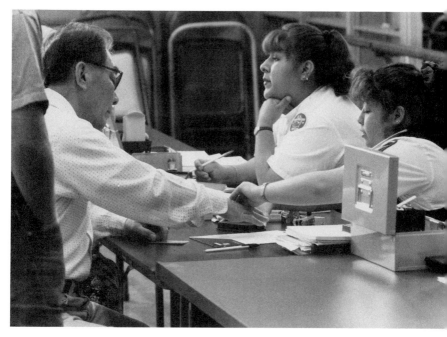

Permanent United States residents with green cards, as well as temporary workers on visas, must now renew their documents. This Santa Barbara, California, man was fingerprinted when the INS issued new permanent resident cards.

The widespread number of illegals working in child care came home to many citizens in 1993 when the new administration's first two selections for Attorney General—the first women ever nominated to the office—withdrew because they had hired illegals as nannies.

Both men and women in the amnesty survey reported working an average of two to five hours a week longer than natives at an hourly wage 60 percent of that of comparable American workers.[22] Many held two jobs. From these wages they were able, in 1987, to send $1.2 billion to family outside the United States. About one in ten reported being paid less than the minimum wage, which was a rate of occurrence five times higher than that generally estimated for all workers.

While some stereotypes fell, others may have been reinforced by the new data. A special agricultural worker amnesty confirmed the size of the pool of illegal migrant farm workers when it drew nearly 1.3 million applications. More than 80 percent were Mexican nationals, most of whom lived in California, Texas, and Florida.[23]

Unfortunately, information is also fragmentary on other social issues involving legal and illegal immigrants, such as how many are getting state and federal benefits, a topic treated in the next chapter.

5

Social Services
and the Immigrant

Adversaries often use the horseshoe magnet metaphor to describe America's appeal to legal and illegal immigrants. One pole is job opportunities and the other is social services such as welfare, health care, and education. Which pole pulls most strongly is a point of much disagreement, with liberals emphasizing jobs and conservatives social services.

Arguments about costs and benefits of social services to immigrants often suffer from too few facts and too many biased assumptions. Frequently, no distinctions are drawn among legal, refugee, and illegal immigrants. What is clear is that the federal tax collection system creates an unequal distribution of funds, with Washington taking the lion's share of immigrants' taxes while state and local governments pay for most of the services they receive.

Legal immigrants and refugees are entitled to different levels of federal support, Congress has decided, while illegals are supposed to get almost no support. Emergency medical care, which is available to any poor person, some maternity care at publicly funded hospitals, and a public education are the main exceptions. Even former illegals granted amnesty are prohibited from receiving most types of public assistance for five years following their change of status.

A green-cardholder enters the country with a work permit and a sponsor who has promised the government that no welfare costs will result from this person's arrival for at least three years. Legal immigrants may be aided by family, church, or privately funded ethnic aid groups, but few public programs single them out for assistance. In 1992, for example, Washington provided $30 million for limited health services to migrant workers, a program first started in 1962. There is also support for education, which will be covered in the next chapter.

The United States helps refugees and asylees train for and find jobs, as well as resettle. Washington funds English classes, and, for the first eight months after arrival, provides medical aid and small cash grants to particularly needy refugee families. New refugees may also qualify for welfare programs open to citizens, such as Aid to Families with Dependent Children (AFDC), old-age assistance, general relief, and Supplemental Security Income.[1]

Where Do Immigrant Taxes Go?

At the state and local levels, especially in those six or seven states with the highest concentrations of immigrants, officials complain that most of the tax revenue from immigrants flows to Washington. While states collect sales, license, income, and property taxes, Washington takes the bulk of income and all Social Security taxes. Local governments' costs to resettle refugees, educate newcomers' children, treat poor people's medical problems, and jail illegals usually exceed any federal aid in these areas.

FAIR compared "the $36 billion that immigrants contribute to welfare to the $56 billion they consume" and concluded that "immigrants consume $20 billion more over their lifetimes than they contribute." No sources were given for this figure. Instead, illegals' costs were cited as indirect support. FAIR claimed that, in 1991, Los Angeles County "provided welfare to 117,000 United States-born children of illegal aliens at a cost of $318 million" and that these children make up 65 percent of the births in county-run hospitals, costing Los Angeles County $28 million a year. Also, California's medical program for the poor estimates annual health care costs for illegal immigrants at $700 million.[2]

In their book *The Immigration Time Bomb,* former Colorado Governor Richard D. Lamm and Gary Imhoff, a researcher for FAIR, said that immigrant use of social services is a problem. "It's hard to know how big the problem is," they wrote, but the United States "cannot ignore the growing burden caused by large numbers of immigrants, particularly illegal aliens." They cited a study by Donald Huddle of illegal immigration that projected costs to United States taxpayers of $25 billion a year in unemployment benefits, social services, and underpayment of taxes. When it comes to legal immigrants, however, who far outnumber the illegals, Lamm and Imhoff admitted there is no solid evidence that they use any more services than a comparable segment of the native-born population.[3]

The Problem with Studies

Study results hinge on what is measured, and few are comprehensive enough to satisfy all sides. In a Los Angeles County study, legal and illegal immigrants generated $4.3 billion in taxes to all levels of government in 1991–1992. They used $2.45 billion in total health, welfare, education, and justice-related services. The county footed 39 percent of the service bill while collecting only 3 percent of the taxes.[4] However, the apparent net contribution of $1.85 billion, some critics said, did not consider all government expenditures in the county. Other critics, who faulted the study for too high costs and too low contributions, pointed out that the accounting methods used would also portray native-born citizens as a net cost to the county.

Time frame is another factor in immigrant studies. "All the focus in recent studies has been on recent immigrants, which fosters the mistaken impression that problems they face the first years . . . [in] the country last indefinitely," explained Urban Institute researcher Rebecca L. Clark.[5]

The National Forum contended that "immigrants are generally young. They come to work, not go on welfare, and they use less social services than United States-born residents."[6] They cited a 1985 Bureau of Labor Statistics report on AFDC and food stamp users. It concluded, "the foreign-born do not seem more likely than the United States-born to be recipients of government benefits."

A 1990 study of immigrants and Social Security by the Alexis de Tocqueville Institution established that most recent contributors do not have parents currently collecting benefits, noted the National Forum. This replenishes Social Security, since by the time the immigrants themselves start collecting benefits, their children are already paying into the system. These examples examined national welfare programs, but immigrant rights advocates recognize the pressure on states and localities.

The Federal vs. State Tussle

"Immigrants pay taxes, but the larger portion of revenue goes to the federal government, and the greater burden associated with immigrants goes to the states," said Cecelia Munoz, immigration expert for the National Council of La Raza, a Latino issues research and advocacy group in Washington, D.C. The problem, she added, is being posed incorrectly as "there shouldn't be immigrants because they're costing money."[7] Indeed, a national poll found that 59 percent of respondents agreed with the assertion that "many immigrants wind up on welfare and raise taxes for Americans."[8]

California Governor Pete Wilson drew widespread support in early 1993 when he presented President Bill Clinton's administration with a $1.45 billion bill for services rendered to refugees and immigrants. Governor Wilson claimed that

$678 million was spent on refugee resettlement, health and welfare costs for legalized immigrants, and to imprison noncitizen criminals. Another $774 million was needed for illegals' emergency medical care and welfare services to their American-born children.[9] The governors of New York, Illinois, Florida, and Texas signed a letter to President Clinton calling for "full reimbursement" for federally-required state services. (Another state complaint has been federal postponement of promised amnesty expense reimbursements.)

Washington responded with more money for illegal immigrants' medical needs. The states did not get all they wanted, partly because to do so would require redrawing United States welfare and medical aid laws. By 1994, Florida, Texas, and California had joined New York in suing the federal government for nonreimbursed costs linked to illegal immigrants.

State Immigrant Aid: Texas and Massachusetts

State and local support for legal immigrants varies widely. The Urban Institute compared Massachusetts and Texas because they represented nearly opposite poles in terms of services and outreach aimed at immigrants.[10] Texas, which had a total 1992 newcomer population (including around 300,000 illegals) of nearly 1.5 million, had no special programs of its own for legal or legalized immigrants and refugees. It spent no state money on refugees except what was required to match federal cash and medical payments. Help for legalized residents was based on what the state expected to be reimbursed under the amnesty law.

Massachusetts, with a total 1992 newcomer population (including about 35,000 illegals) of a little more than 300,000 temporarily offered an assistance program to about thirty cities and towns impacted by immigrants. Nearly $20 million was spent between 1987 and 1991 on legal, education, and community services for non-English speakers. Legal services, primarily for undocumented asylum-seekers, continue to be funded, but a souring economy and anti-immigrant backlash

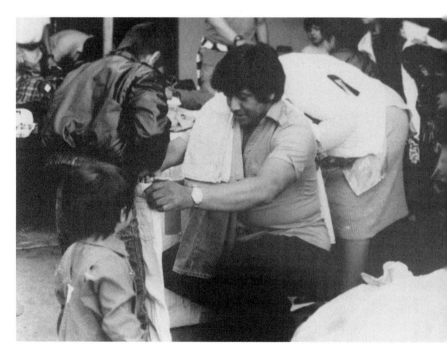

The Guatemalan father of two boys sizes them for donated clothes at a nonprofit Los Angeles refugee relief center. A backlog of 300,000 asylum claims comes mostly from Central Americans living in the Los Angeles area.

have eliminated special services and cut the state's general assistance, a welfare program for all poor people.

Unlike other immigrants, refugees can quickly qualify for welfare. Their residency patterns hint that higher benefit levels may promote migration from state to state, but are not the sole reason for any moving that they do. Texas, which has long paid lower welfare benefits than most states, lost 982 refugees in 1986 while Massachusetts gained 1,170 and California 7,886. In 1990, however, the pattern changed, and Texas, with a growing economy, had more net refugee migration than the other two states. This suggested to Urban Institute researchers that secondary migration may be encouraged by job opportunities, family, and ethnic communities as well as welfare payments.[11]

Illegals' Use of the System

Illegal immigrants, like most people who do not have health insurance, wait until they become seriously ill before seeking care. This costs the public heavily in emergency medical services. Annual spending on illegals through Medicaid, the federal–state medical cost-sharing program for the poor, rose 160 percent in recession-wracked California between 1989 and 1992. The state's share jumped from $300 million to $783 million during that time.[12] But this amounted to just 6.4 percent of the state's total Medicaid costs in 1992.

To protect the public from contagious diseases, as well as to reassure illegals, state rules had forbid health care workers from asking recipients of Medicaid to prove their eligibility.

Until the California Legislature recently closed this loophole, ill nonimmigrants who lied about being poor and illegal could get free medical care, while illegals got the blame.

Many illegals, according to information provided by amnesty participants, generally paid for their hospital care themselves or with private insurance. Only 4 percent got free care and 21 percent reported receiving help from Medicaid or Medicare (federal aid for the elderly).[13] The same survey showed that families applying for amnesty in 1988 and 1989 were half as likely as the general population to be receiving food stamps or AFDC, and one-fifth as likely to be getting unemployment benefits. They were twice as likely to receive some form of state welfare as natives, if their state offered any general assistance.[14]

Early Immigrants' Medical Care

Contrary to current impressions, early immigrants also received a form of publicly funded medical care. New York City's receiving station at Castle Garden, which was built by the state in 1855, had a small hospital for minor illnesses. Major cases went to another state-run immigrant medical facility on Ward's Island. Other ports of entry had similar, if smaller, medical operations.

Author Barbara Benton found no coincidence in the fact that "the first welfare system in the world was established in New York, not as a result of a particularly liberal point of view, but out of dire need."[15] New York State, at the end of the nineteenth century, spent $20 million annually on care for the insane and the poor, some of whom were recent immigrants.

Immigration now, as then, is a decision made by families as well as individuals. Educational opportunity was crucial in this decision, and the impact of non-English-speaking children is a problem that echoes in today's school corridors.

chapter

6

Educating
the Immigrant

Claremont, California, teenager Karen Felzer was in seventh grade when she realized that a classmate, named Grace, was an immigrant. One day, Karen heard her friend speaking Chinese and learned that she had been born in Taiwan. "I had thought that an immigrant could only be someone's grandparent, not another kid," Karen admitted.[1] Grace taught Chinese words and phrases to Karen at lunch breaks. Soon Karen's circle of friends included many Asian young people.

Former Vietnamese refugee Quyen Tuong Nguyen vividly remembers her first day in a United States high school: "How frightened I was! The students were so tall and handsome."[2] She also recalls feeling a bit embarrassed that she had to join a special line for the free school lunch, for which she qualified because of her family's low income and refugee status.

Free or discounted meals are one of the few federal benefits available to immigrant students. This program is actually an antipoverty effort and many recent immigrant families are poor. The government halted funding of a special program for refugee students in 1989, but it has continued a smaller, more general aid program mandated by the Emergency Immigrant Education Act (EIEA). The $30 million allotted newcomers under EIEA in 1990 amounted to $42 for each student, half of what was being spent six years earlier.[3] School districts used most of this money for teacher training, books, study aids, and other instructional expenses. Another modest federal program helps educate children of migrant workers.

An Obligation to Educate

Most federal aid to immigrant students comes in the form of general antipoverty efforts or aid to bilingual education. Overall, United States spending on bilingual programs is estimated at $175 to $200 million annually. Adjusted for inflation, this represents a drop of almost 50 percent in federal bilingual funding during the 1980s—while the number of school students with limited English proficiency, known as LEP, rose by 50 percent.[4]

Legal immigrants may also qualify for federal scholarships, loans, or work-study programs to help them attend college or trade schools. Illegal immigrants are not eligible for such loans and grants, but the United States Supreme Court has said that the Constitution guarantees free public elementary and secondary schooling to all children, whatever their immigration status. LEP students are entitled by law to special help in learning English and making progress in other subjects. These legal mandates seldom enjoy adequate state and federal aid, leaving most urban school districts, where immigrants concentrate, chronically underfunded.

Not everyone complies fully with the court rulings. Georgia required students to have a valid Social Security number to be able to enroll in school, a move that blocks public schooling for the children of illegals.[5] Access to higher education and its cost to illegal noncitizens also varies among the states. Following state court rulings, California charges illegals out-of-state tuition if they enroll at any community college or University of California campus. Maryland immigrants are allowed a break on in-state tuition if they work for certain international organizations.[6]

Where the Newcomer Kids Are

Foreign-born youth accounted for 3 percent of the under-eighteen segment of the population in the 1990 census. For school-age children and young adults, this meant a little more than 2 million immigrant students enrolled in United States schools during the 1980s. Underscoring the general imbalance in immigrant distribution, 78 percent of all recent newcomer students attend schools in only five states: California, New York, Texas, Illinois, and Florida.[7] With 270,000 of these newcomers in 1990, California had more than twice as many as New York, the next most impacted state.

In Texas, where the Latino population rose 45 percent in the 1980s, pressure for school reforms sparked lawsuits over state educational aid formulas. One result was the so-called Robin Hood reform, a plan that took revenues from rich districts to give to poorer ones. Commenting on $47 million that Dallas lost to districts in south Texas, newspaper columnist Richard Estrada blamed the resulting political controversy on Latino growth. "High birthrates and immigration from Mexico and Central America are key growth factors in many state school districts," wrote *The Dallas Morning News* associate editor.[8]

With nearly 1 million students, New York City has the nation's largest school system. The population had declined to 918,000 in the early 1980s, and school officials attributed the recent rebound as mostly due to immigrants. Immigrant students arriving between 1989 and 1992 comprised nearly 14 percent of enrollment.[9] Bilingual program costs run to $650 a year for each student. Puerto Ricans, who are United States citizens, make up nearly 40 percent of New York City's students. They are largely Spanish-speaking and often need bilingual classes.

Large numbers are only part of the new immigrants' impact on some school districts; another aspect is the students' diversity, particularly in languages. A few examples: New York City students represent 188 nationalities; Washington, D.C., schools count 127 languages among their pupils, while in nearby Arlington, Virginia, school students speak 59 different languages, including Farsi (Iranian) and Khmer (Cambodian); Miami, with plenty of Cuban-American teachers, has no shortage of Spanish-speaking instructors but needs French

Creole speakers to cope with the surge of new Haitian refugee children; most of Los Angeles Unified School District's 280,000 limited-English speakers use Spanish, but 79 other languages are also present in the schools.

With an eye on spiraling enrollments and state funding cuts, FAIR warns, "By continuing immigration at unprecedented levels, we are overburdening our schools, which are struggling to provide even a basic education to our children, much less prepare them to compete in the world economy of the future."[10] The anti-immigrant group says that in 1992 it cost $45 million for just Dade County, Florida, to educate the one out of every four students who was a new immigrant.

The English-Only Movement

Immigrants cost Americans more than money, argues U.S.ENGLISH, a national lobby against bilingual education and multilingual ballots. "English is under attack," says the group, which sees the growth of the non-English-speaking population, especially Spanish speakers, as a threat to American unity: "Record immigration, concentrated in fewer language groups, is reinforcing language segregation and retarding language assimilation."[11] The lobby, which was launched in 1983 by a former United States senator and one of FAIR's founders, seeks a constitutional amendment that makes English the official language of the United States, and bars public services in other languages. It claimed 400,000 members in 1988.

The National Forum does not dispute the high costs of educating children who are often poor and, by definition, from a different cultural and (usually) language background. But, it holds, America ignores these students' education or their special language needs at its peril. Forum members fought for the legal mandate for such services. They also promote a more equal return of tax dollars to impacted school districts, but they reject charges that recent immigrants are resisting learning English and are assimilating more slowly than previous newcomers.

"In fact," said Forum Executive Director Frank Sharry, "in keeping with the pattern of [earlier] European immigrants . . . most recently arrived adult immigrants have limited English ability, while their children are bilingual, and their grandchildren speak fluent English (while only half learn . . . Spanish)."[12]

A 1990 Latino National Political Survey of more than 2,800 citizens of Mexican, Cuban, and Puerto Rican descent supported Sharry's general scenario, finding that two-thirds of American-born Latinos speak better English than Spanish. The survey revealed that 90 percent of respondents believed that if you live in the United States you should learn to speak English. Though there were differences among the groups, most did not support increased immigration. At the same time, large majorities disagreed with English-only measures, favored bilingual services, and said that teaching English should be bilingual education's major goal.[13]

Cross Fire over Bilingual Programs

Bilingual education, which comes in several forms, is the main way in which states and schools teach skills to students who have little or no English knowledge. In schools, the debate is over teaching students subjects in their native language while they gradually learn English, or teaching almost exclusively in English and making them sink or swim. A severe shortage of bilingual teachers has forced many districts to use the latter approach, despite the higher dropout rate associated with it. Outside the classroom, the debate over bilingualism has grown shrill.

What children will learn from teachers in bilingual programs concerns George Tryfiates, executive director of English First, a group allied with U.S.ENGLISH in fighting for an English-only America. English First also opposes instruction that the United States is a land of many cultures. In a letter to supporters, Tryfiates suggested their children "may soon be taught that America is a hateful place founded by racists and murderers . . . [or] that they are descendants of the European 'ice people' whose lack of skin color identifies them as an inferior race! . . . Many of these educational 'experts' are also behind the drive for so-called 'bilingualism.' I put it in quotes because these people really want to do away with English and everything European." [14]

Tryfiates and others in the English-only movement have tasted success. Constitutional amendments or special statutes to make English the official state language passed in seventeen states. In the United States territory of Puerto Rico, both English and Spanish are official languages. But a common language is not always the beautiful bond it's made out to be. British playwright George Bernard Shaw wryly noted this when he said, "England and America are two countries divided by the same language."

Schools are powerful instruments for the integration of newcomers into American society, exposing them to negative and positive experiences. Drug use and violence in schools are often the subjects of news reports. Less frequently noted are lessons like the one learned by Armenian émigré Ofelya Bagdasaryan. When she pulled a D on her first college exam, she told the grader, "But I repeated exactly what the textbook said."

"Yes," he replied, "but you didn't tell us your opinion of what the book said."[15]

Independent thinking was not encouraged in the former Soviet system, nor in many other nations' educational systems for that matter. On the other hand, teachers command respect in Asian and Latin American societies, and this is reflected in immigrants' initial classroom punctuality and behavior. Most instructors enjoy working with newcomers and reportedly regret that after a few years most have adapted to native-born peer behavior.[16]

Many newcomers have problems beyond that of language education. Teachers find some new students have had no schooling before and, in rare cases, do not even know how to hold a pencil; they may be taken out of class by their parents for long periods, interrupting instruction. They may have never seen a doctor, nor a dentist, nor had an eye exam.[17] Some suffer from fleeing war-ravaged countries or from being separated from their parents for years. Few schools are equipped to deal with such problems.

These are some of the challenges and rewards schools face with today's immigrants, but society's responses may not be all that new. As historian George Pozzetta has noted, "America responded to the immigrant presence [in the past] in varied ways. During periods of crisis, the host society often reacted by promoting rigid programs of Americanization that sought to strip away foreign customs and values. . . . Immigrants . . . frequently reacted to these initiatives with caution and skepticism."[18]

Such reactions are probably as common today as they were at the turn of the century.

7

Immigrants and Assimilation: Making a New Home

Joseph C. Spencer, Jr., was in the aisle of his favorite Miami supermarket when he had a head-on encounter with cultural assimilation. This is how he tells the story: "While I was grocery-shopping for a Fourth of July party, my supermarket cart bumped one pushed by a Hispanic man. I speak no Spanish and evidently he spoke no English, so we smiled apologetically at each other.

"I looked at the contents of his cart—hot dogs, hamburgers, rolls, potato chips, ketchup, and coleslaw—and his eyes followed mine. Then he motioned to my cart, and we burst out laughing. I had selected tortillas, avocados, chili peppers, and refried beans."[1]

Assimilation is a two-way process. It enriches the host society as well as the newcomer, if both sides are receptive. In this case, shared foods, an important and traditional benefit of cultural exchange, was less important than shared laughter. There are many ups and downs in the immigration and assimilation processes that bring pain and tears to the immigrant as well as pleasure and joy. Economic and educational opportunities expand, personal freedom often increases, but the costs go beyond the rigors of getting to America and winning legal permission to work and live here.

Social scientists say adjustments are inevitable, whether or not the immigrant becomes a citizen. Usually one needs to learn a new language, to cope with poverty's crippling effects, to handle changes within the family, and to find ways to live with a new culture that may be confusing, threatening, and at odds with the immigrant's old ways of doing things.

Still a Melting Pot?

Language can be a major cause of isolation for newcomers, retarding economic progress and turning family relationships upside down. Lack of English may deprive educated adults of careers, forcing them into what they consider menial work. In many cultures, it is embarrassing and demeaning for parents to rely on their children as interpreters; it may threaten their authority.

The 1990 census found that one in seven United States residents spoke a language other than English at home. City-dwellers over age five who did not speak English very well constituted almost half the population of Miami, 30 percent of Los Angeles, one-quarter of San Francisco, one-fifth of

New York and San Antonio. In Houston, Chicago, and Boston they accounted for 15 percent or less of total residents.[2]

Though not yet the urban majority, large groups of non-English-speaking people stir old fears. One recent national poll asked if the United States was still the traditional melting pot of cultures or whether today's immigrants strongly maintained their old identities. About two-thirds of the responses said that national identities dominated while only 20 percent felt the melting pot still reigned. When respondents were asked which of several geographic groups should be encouraged to immigrate, Eastern Europeans had the most support, but none won majority approval.[3]

Eastern Europeans were among those whom Massachusetts Senator Henry Cabot Lodge wanted to bar in 1896. He urged a test for literacy because it "will bear most heavily upon the Italians, Russians, Poles, Hungarians, Greeks, and Asiatics. . . . In other words, the races most affected by the illiteracy test are those whose emigration to this country has begun within the last twenty years and swelled rapidly to enormous proportions, races which the English-speaking people have never hitherto assimilated. . . ."[4]

Race prejudice endures as an obstacle to assimilation and adds to the immigrant's ordeal. In earlier eras, Anglos objected to people who "looked foreign," and often refused to hire them because of their names. The experience of a successful Czech caterer in an unidentified United States city seemed typical to a social worker in 1934. The elite, he told her, would not do business with him until after he changed his name. He said that act "nearly killed my father, but he now sees it was necessary."[5]

The struggle to be accepted continues, but today's immigrant faces are more often Asian or Latin than Slavic or Anglo. Blending in cannot be achieved by changing a name or an accent. But in some cities, enough people of the same nationality or ethnic group exist to form a community, making rejection less painful and possibly softening the assimilation process.

Ethnic Communities

Lost in a world of incomprehensible sounds before they learn English, people who speak the same tongue usually live together for mutual relief and protection. These enclaves offer a sense of the familiar, even reuniting neighbors from the same native regions. Enclaves can provide housing, religious and social life, and jobs for some, or at least work contacts in a known ethnic network. They may re-create old political and class divisions, but they also help buffer an outsider against the strangeness of the new land. As older Latino barrios, Little Tokyos, and Chinatowns filled up, or did not welcome recent émigrés, new enclaves blossomed. They were usually in run-down residential and business districts; sometimes, new immigrants took over older enclaves.

Chicago's Vietnamese created a prosperous Little Saigon in the Uptown district, which was known in the mid-1970s for drug dealing, burned-out storefronts, and muggings. In Miami, the once all-Anglo Sweetwater area is mostly Nicaraguan and the heavily Cuban suburb of Hialeah now has a Haitian section.

Over a span of two decades, Los Angeles grew a Koreatown in its Wilshire district, only to see parts of it destroyed in the 1992 riots. New York City's Little Italy is now predominantly Chinese while Puerto Ricans, once the controlling Latino group, have ceded territory to Dominicans and Colombians.

Geographic concentration increases immigrants' visibility and magnifies their impact on everything from schools, public housing, transportation, and medical services to foreign-language television, radio, and advertising. To some native-born Americans, the impacts are dangerous. One member of an anti-immigrant group described a visit to downtown Los Angeles this way: "It was another country. Hispanic immigrants were having a *paseo,* walking on the sidewalk, eyeing each other, playing loud music. I felt displaced and alienated."[6]

Others, even if they like the diversity of the enclaves, feel that they threaten national unity. "When these immigrants do not learn English and rely solely on what their small community can provide for them," warns U.S.ENGLISH supporter Fernando de la Peña, "it often results in the creation of a permanent economic and social underclass. These people will never gain many of the advantages available to them in the larger community. . . . They are ripe for social unrest and become the easy prey of unscrupulous vultures, from drug lords to religious leaders."[7]

Adds U.S.ENGLISH spokeswoman Cessna Winslow, "Our opponents say we're racists. We're not racists. We feel by . . . discouraging someone from learning the common tongue, you're denying them the opportunities to really enjoy America."

Changes in the Assimilation Game

Some conservative critics, like *Forbes* magazine editor Peter Brimelow, contend that though previous immigrants, who also lived in enclaves, ended up becoming assimilated, the ground rules have changed for the worse. "Earlier waves of immigrants were basically free to succeed or fail," Brimelow argued—about one-third of the 1880–1920 émigrés returned home—but state welfare and multiculturalism policies have undermined the traditional sorting-out process.

He charges that these policies promote Latino separateness. "The various groups of Spanish-speaking immigrants are now much less encouraged to assimilate to American culture," he claimed. An English immigrant himself, Brimelow derided "the drive to transform America from a nation into a charity ward," and blamed public policies such as "official bilingualism . . . multilingual ballots; defining citizenship so as to include all children born here—even children of illegals; the abandonment of English as a prerequisite for citizenship; . . . the extension of welfare and education benefits as a right to illegals and their children; congressional and state legislative apportionment based on legal and illegal populations."[8]

Conservative columnist George F. Will, who judges immigrants as an asset overall, thought that "a welfare culture . . . weakens the mainspring of individual striving for upward mobility." He does not blame the immigrants for "the weakening of the ideal of assimilation." For that he turns to "those native-born intellectuals who believe America is a sick, racist, sexist, exploitative, oppressive, patriarchal society."[9] His tongue-in-cheek solution: Deport one unhappy tenured professor for every ten immigrants.

But is the drive toward assimilation weakening? The National Forum rejects the idea, pointing to studies of English acquisition among immigrants. Noting improvement in English language skills from generation to generation, the pro-immigrant coalition said, "By the third generation, the original language is lost, fostering the ironic need for the vast majority of United States college students to learn a second language."

A Glimpse at Naturalization

Changes in the rate at which permanent residents become naturalized citizens might indicate speed of assimilation. The bulk of those who naturalize do so in eight years, a median time span that has not changed between 1960 and 1990. But the naturalization rate of a given group has been little studied. An INS analysis of immigrants admitted in 1977 found that 37.4 percent had become citizens by 1990. Though this was a lower rate than some expected, it may be skewed by the group's large number of Cuban exiles, many of whom hope to return to their homeland. So far as adding new citizens, each decade since 1960 has marked an increase. Total naturalizations climbed from 1.1 million in 1961–1970 to 2.4 million in 1981–1990.[10]

No solid answers to questions about cultural change in America can be expected for some time. Despite fragmentation fears or hopes of forming a multicultural society, a lot of what happens depends on the way Americans go about their daily lives. Historian Daniel J. Boorstein put it this way: "There has been so much emphasis recently on the diversity of our peoples. I think it's time we reaffirmed the fact that what built our country is community, and that community . . . is dependent on the willingness of people to build together."[11]

Ethnic pride has enjoyed a rebirth in America, and coping with cultural diversity is a social goal. But the resulting tugs and pulls from different directions can add to the individual's ordeal. As fifteen-year-old Julie Lee, a Korean American from Los Angeles, phrased it in a poem:

> *Stranger, brother sister, I am you from far away. Come here and stand by me.*[12]

The number of naturalized citizens, who must learn a certain level of English to pass their tests, is one measure of assimilation. About half of all new Americans since 1981 have come from Asian homelands.

8

Crime and
the Immigrant

When conservative columnist Patrick Buchanan ran against
George Bush for the Republican party's 1992 presidential
nomination, he frequently linked immigrants to crime rates.
Buchanan warned that "our great cities are riven with gang
wars among Asian, black, and Hispanic youth who grow
up to run ethnic crime cartels."[1] If immigrants did not
create crime problems, they surely fueled their growth, he
argued.

These attacks prompted Warren R. Leiden, executive
director of the American Immigration Lawyers Association,
to warn: "Buchanan's scapegoating of immigrants for America's social problems may win the fear, anxiety, and hatred
vote, but the division he sows will surely hurt the vast
majority of Americans and chip away at traditional American
values."[2]

After the spring 1992 riots in Los Angeles, a director of
FAIR linked that violence, not to outrage over perceived racial

injustice or mob frenzy, but to immigration: "Massive immigration widens the divide between wealth and poverty, storing up social dynamite, especially diminishing life for African Americans."[3] Response to these assertions was sharp.

Representatives of two San Francisco-based coalitions of civil and immigrant rights groups charged that "when healing should have been our national priority, FAIR shamelessly attempted to exploit the raw tensions and pit against each other the two groups it most despises: immigrants and poor American-born people of color."

Fear of Crime

In early 1993, FAIR published a paper on asylum reform that spoke to fears stirred by the rash of criminal activity mentioned in Chapter 1. "The chief suspects in the murders at the gate of the CIA headquarters and in the bombing of the World Trade Center are aliens who appear to have abused our asylum laws only to turn their terror on the country that naively extended a hand of hospitality and welcome to them," it said in part. "These incidents, not to mention common sense, tell us that our immigration and asylum laws and procedures need to be changed in the interests of public safety and protection of our society."[4]

Many participants in the debate over immigration, including President Clinton, agree that asylum abuse must be stopped, but they resist tarring all immigrants with certain individuals' violent acts. A major problem is that little objective data, and even less analysis, are available to help define what sociologists call "new immigrant crime."[5] Most local police departments do not note the citizenship status of people they arrest, and some cities refuse to help the INS find and prosecute illegal immigrants.

However, blaming vulnerable, usually powerless groups for social and economic ills is a standard feature of the American political landscape. It goes back at least to the nativists of the last century, particularly when the charge is crime.

Senator Henry Cabot Lodge, in pushing for immigrant literacy tests in 1896, claimed his statistics "prove that illiteracy runs parallel with the slum populations, with criminals, paupers, and juvenile delinquents of foreign birth or parentage. . . ."[6] In the late 1920s, President Herbert Hoover wrote then-New York Congressman Fiorello La Guardia that Italians are "predominantly our murderers and bootleggers . . . foreign spawn [who] do not appreciate this country."[7] The racism is less blatant today, but vicious stereotypes are often based on isolated instances, and unrelated facts can be bent to create the appearance of truth.

Fear of crime and random violence is widespread in America. Combine this with high-profile ethnic criminal activity in some cities, whether or not it involves noncitizens, and immigrant opponents may seize upon an apparent issue.

"One of the consequences of ceasing to enforce sensible immigration controls has been the wave of alien-related crime that has struck our nation from coast to coast," charged a 1988 book sponsored by The American Immigration Control Foundation (AICF), an anti-immigrant group.[8] The authors cited as support some nationalities involved in mostly drug-related organized crime; they did not mention any contradictory evidence.

Increased street gang activity, including that of immigrant gangs in New York, Chicago, Miami, Newark, and Los Angeles, has drawn FBI and INS attention. But felony crimes have also decreased in some immigrant-impacted cities. Two years of falling crime figures cheered officials of New York City, where one-quarter of all residents are foreign-born. In 1991, 72 percent of police precincts reported declines; the next year

Illegal immigrants crossing from Mexico are the U.S. Border Patrol's main target, but the patrol is also on the lookout for drug smugglers.

felonies dropped in 90 percent of the city's seventy-five precincts. Murders fell below 2,000 for the first time since 1989. Queens' heavily immigrant Elmhurst district, which may be "the most ethnically mixed community in the world," saw felonies decline 7.7 percent in one year.[9]

The Cuban Mariellos

The AICF authors emphasized violence attributed to some of the *Mariellos,* the 125,000 people Cuban President Fidel Castro released in a massive boat-lift to Florida in 1980. The Mariello criminals, however, are a special case, unrepresentative of Cubans or immigrants generally. Mixed with the legitimate Cuban refugees accepted by President Jimmy Carter were convicts and mentally ill people who had been deliberately loaded onto the boats. Officials put them at 2,500; unofficial estimates ranged up to 40,000.[10]

Whatever the actual number, it is widely agreed that America's humane welcome brought grief to many. Miami's crime rate soared and soon other United States cities felt the sting of Cuban criminals. Union City, a Cuban center in New Jersey, laid one-third of all felonies in the mid-1980s at the Mariellos' door. Las Vegas law officials estimated one-quarter of their Cuban refugees were career criminals.[11] Federal prison inmates and guards suffered when imprisoned Mariellos rioted in 1987 after it was announced that they would be returned to Cuba.

More than 100,000 Mariellos finally settled in America. But legal battles swirled around approximately 1,800 inmates whom INS held in detention for more than a decade after their arrival. Judged by courts as having few United States rights, the detainees had to prove they were fit for release after serving their sentences.[12] Few could do so. Castro has now agreed to take back most of the imprisoned Mariellos, leaving their United States legal status unresolved.

Mariello gangsters provide a strong example of negative impacts of federal immigration policy at state and local levels. But they and other ethnic career criminals hardly prove AICF's contention that "there is scarcely a community in

Anti-immigrant groups urge more drastic law enforcement measures against illegals than the steps supported by pro-immigrant organizations. Nearly everyone, however, favors building up the U.S. Border Patrol, seen here preparing to take away an illegal captured on the southern border.

America that has gone untouched by alien-related crime—a crime-wave which will continue to worsen unless strong action is taken."[13]

Paying for Flawed Policies

Fallout from flawed federal policies taints other parts of America's justice system. The growing cost of maintaining illegal noncitizens in state prisons prompted New York State to sue the United States in 1992. The state claimed that federal law required the INS to take custody of illegals who have served prison time and are eligible for parole. New York asserted that it cost around $100 million to house 3,400 such inmates for a year. California, home to half of the estimated United States illegal population of 3.2 million, and Texas, also host to a large group of illegals, are closely watching the case. With 17,000 illegals in its prisons, California figures support costs run as high as $500 million annually.

The federal prison system, which calculates that illegals already represent 26 percent of its population, says it has neither resources nor mandate to shoulder the states' burden. INS does deport criminals, more than 15,000 in 1992, and about half of them had narcotics violations.[14] Some in Congress urged speeding up the deportation process; others want to convert closed military bases into prisons for the illegals. The latter proposal rouses immigrant advocates' fears that some illegals could be condemned to the legal limbo that kept Mariellos in cells long after they had served their sentences.

Law Enforcement and the Illegals

Illegal immigrants, even if they are not convicted criminals, are a border problem and a major stress on law enforcement and other social resources. They may be Mexicans dashing across the southern border under cover of night, or Italians arriving in a New York City airport without documents, or shiploads of Polish or Chinese illegals being intercepted by the Coast Guard. For various reasons, millions have decided not to wait for legal permission to find jobs and homes in the United States.

Packing people like sardines in a can is one way smugglers increase their profits. This rental truck was carrying twenty-eight illegals when it was stopped. Estimates of the nation's permanent illegal population vary from 3 to 6 million people.

Reliable numbers are hard to come by, as can be expected of people who fear deportation if identified. The Border Patrol stopped illegal border-crossers about 1.2 million times in 1991 and 1992. Though higher than some years, this total is lower than the peak of 1.8 million apprehensions in 1986.[15] However, the number of apprehensions does not equal the number of different individuals because many of those captured are repeat offenders.

Estimates of the current permanent illegal population run from 3 to 6 million people, with the INS accepting the figure at the lower end of the spectrum. (Some anti-immigrant sources still use 12 million, a discredited number from the 1970s.) California claims it harbors as many as 2 million illegals, most of them living in the southern counties. New York State has about half a million, with 80 percent living in New York City. The nationality mix varies greatly among states. Mexico was the single largest supplier of illegals to California and Texas, but failed to make New York's top twenty contributors.[16] Ecuador, Italy, and Poland provided the most illegal nationals living in New York in 1992.

INS says it cannot estimate how many illegals enter annually, but the Census Bureau figures their net growth at 200,000. FAIR maintains that 300,000 are permanent settlers. No one knows how many illegals who have slipped past the Border Patrol return home each year, especially when home is the other side of a 2,000-mile southern border. Illegals cross the 3,500-mile northern border, too, but only 1.5 percent of 1992 apprehensions were along the northern tier. Few people voice concern over this immigrant route, though the INS thinks more than 100,000 Canadians are living illegally in the United States.[17]

To many experts, the problem represented by illegals is more basic than whether or not they come for jobs or services or both. One think tank, the Brookings Institution of Washington, D.C., concluded: "Illegal immigration deserves attention because it is a massive violation of law that has the effect of distorting the objectives of the country's immigration policy with respect to the size and composition of the immigrant stream; it contributes to an array of other illegal acts [like fake papers]. . . ."[18]

Border Patrol vs. the Smugglers

In 1992, illegal drugs became a major part of the Border Patrol's antismuggling responsibilities. While INS statistics do not identify the citizenship status of drug smugglers, they estimate the street value of annual seizures at around $1.6 to $1.75 billion between 1990 and 1992.[19] At the same time, INS field agents charge that smuggling people across United States borders is even bigger business. They report that Asian organized crime gangs alone haul in around $3 billion annually by sneaking ethnic Chinese from Vietnam, Taiwan, and mainland China into the United States.[20]

Many illegal Asians take the southern route and follow Mexican guides, called coyotes, into the United States where compatriot smugglers reclaim them. The illegal émigrés are taken to safe houses in Los Angeles and other southwestern cities, while their families are often squeezed for more money. Fees ranging up to $30,000 per person have been reported for some Asian illegals. When their families cannot pay, the illegals face years of working off the debt.

Immigrant advocates contend that illegals are more often crime victims than perpetrators. Employers may take advantage of their fears of *la Migra* (the INS) and lack of English to get below-minimum wage, unresisting labor. Though illegals do have rights, and such employers face fines, the immigrants

Smuggling people across international borders can involve elaborate schemes, such as this false bottom on a van, and costs run accordingly. Some Asian illegals have paid $30,000 or more to get into the United States.

constantly worry that all they have built can disappear if their status is discovered. They are easy marks for con artists posing as immigration experts who try to sell them documents that are supposed to legalize their status.

New legal immigrants are also prey for other immigrants who use common ethnic ties to con them. Millions have been lost in what police call affinity scams. Though such con games have been around since the first immigrants walked off the boat, today's versions are more subtle. They often employ modern technology or mind-boggling paperwork to hide fraudulent intent. That happened in New York, where some 1,200 East European immigrant investors lost at least $34 million to a prominent Polish businessman who reached them on Polish-language television. In 1991, he was fined $15 million, sentenced to five years in prison, and ordered to repay all his investors.[21]

The Debate Continues

Tiny Ellis Island, the gateway to America for 12 million settlers, once was considered a poor relation to its glamorous New York Upper Bay neighbor, the Statue of Liberty. During its life as New York's and the nation's main immigrant receiving station, from 1892 to 1954, poets said that Liberty symbolized sweet hope and Ellis grim reality. Emma Lazarus proclaimed the statue "Mother of Exiles," and in 1903 her stirring words, imbedded in bronze, were attached to the statue's base:[1]

> Give me your tired, your poor,
> Your huddled masses yearning to breathe free,
> The wretched refuse of your teeming shore.
> Send these, the homeless, tempest-tost to me,
> I lift my lamp beside the golden door!

Ellis Island proved to be an ugly duckling. It took years, and lots of citizen support, but America's symbolic gateway has been reborn as a powerful, vital museum dedicated to immigrants as nation-builders. Academic leader Peter Sammartino, a member of New Jersey's Bicentennial Commission, mounted the rescue from decades of decay by gathering funds so that the National Park Service could open Ellis Island to visitors for the 1976 U.S. Bicentennial.[2]

Public response paved the way to a federally created Statue of Liberty–Ellis Island Foundation, headed by automaker Lee Iacocca. This group raised $360 million in citizen, foundation, and corporate donations to transform and maintain the national monument sitting between Jersey City and Manhattan. Both Iacocca and Sammartino were sons of Ellis Island sojourners. They knew the red-and-white brick facility was integral to America's past and her ongoing present, a key to understanding the dynamic nature of the American character.

After a seven-year effort, the doors reopened in the fall of 1990 as the Ellis Island Immigration Museum and resource center. The 100,000-square-foot main building and restored grounds are designed to bring the immigrant experience alive with images and voices.[3] It was an immediate success, attracting almost 2 million visitors in its first year.

Coincidentally, the most sweeping immigration reform act in two decades was signed into law at about the same time. But outside Washington, D.C., old fears cast shadows over immigrants; not all are seen as national assets. A 1990 opinion survey sponsored by FAIR found that 48 percent of respondents thought the United States accepts too many immigrants. Two years later, a repeat poll indicated that 54 percent felt too many immigrants were allowed into the country. Eighty-six percent agreed that the United States had an overpopulation problem.[4]

Looking into the Crystal Ball

In 1990, the foreign-born amounted to 8.5 percent of the people living in America; this segment had produced about one-third of the nation's population growth over the previous decade.[5] The percentage was higher in a few regions, such as

As the debate over the impact of current immigrants on America spreads, some perspective can be found in the Ellis Island Immigration Museum.

southern California or Miami–Dade County. Opponents to immigration saw this growth as a danger to America. Their underlying concern was how quickly changes in the United States ethnic mix were trimming the white majority.

The AICF made a call to arms out of its alarm: "[There is an] immigration time bomb planted in the heart of America; a bomb which comes closer to detonating every day. Unless we—the American citizens and our elected representatives—disarm this bomb, it will explode and destroy the United States we know and love."[6]

In 1993, the Census Bureau projected current ethnic growth trends, including immigration, fifty-seven years into the future. The Bureau's numbers are based on assumptions about birth and death rates of different groups as well as on how many people permanently come into or leave the country. In its scenario, the non-Hispanic white portion drops from 76 percent to 68 percent by 2010. In another forty years, the population reaches 392 million and is predicted to be 53 percent white, 23 percent Hispanic, 16 percent black, and 10 percent Asian–Pacific Islander. (By Census Bureau definition, Hispanics can be of any race.)

While agreeing that American ethnic diversity is growing, National Forum members see opportunities and choices in this fact. They issued a statement after the Los Angeles riots that said, in part, "This increasing diversity presents American society with a simple choice. We can deal with the challenges facing our communities constructively, by promoting cooperation and tolerance, or we can permit our fears and prejudices to be exploited by those who seek to divide us."[7] They chose, they said, to seek unity through tolerance and cooperation.

It's unclear how much weight to give demographic projections stretching forward more than half a century. Some studies have shown that certain immigrant women's fertility rates are remarkably similar to those of native-born women in the same age group—even before they leave their homeland.[8] After a few years in the United States, the similarity increases, though the reason for this is unknown. If these results prove to be the rule rather than the exception, conventional projections are useless.

Population Growth and the Environment

Anti-immigrant politicians and groups usually concentrate their fire on what newcomers supposedly cost society while proponents emphasize their estimated benefits. These differences show up over long-standing issues, such as jobs, health care, welfare use, crowding in schools and housing, and crime rates. More recently, opponents have added deteriorating ecosystems to immigrant impacts, mostly because, in this view, any population growth is tied to environmental destruction. Specific examples of immigrant-induced deterioration are usually missing.

Former American neo-Nazi and Ku Klux Klan leader David Duke found Louisiana white voters responsive in 1991 when he attacked immigrants for straining social systems and ecosystems.[9] His failed quest to become governor drew 40 percent of the vote, and won endorsement from the state's highest National Wildlife Federation official.

FAIR, which stresses immigration as the most controllable factor in population growth, says in its literature: "We must take a realistic look at what has happened to this society in the last three decades of massive, unprecedented legal and illegal immigration. We must then move toward establishing policies which will help prevent overpopulation, stop deterioration of the American standard of living, and reduce cultural fragmentation and ethnic tension."[10] California provided fertile ground for cultivating support for FAIR's approach.

In 1992, FAIR joined with the national Population and Environment Balance organization, Californians for Population Stabilization, and the San Francisco chapter of the Sierra Club to raise ecology–population issues in the state. The new allies asked Governor Pete Wilson to set "a population growth rate that is environmentally sustainable" for development in California.

San Francisco civil and immigrant rights groups warned that FAIR had a racist agenda and was using a divide-and-conquer strategy on environmentalists. In reaction, they formed their own coalition with environmental advocates, including other Sierra Club chapters, arguing that the United States needs to control consumption, not divert attention to supposed newcomer impacts on ecosystems.

Proposed Solutions

FAIR has urged specific measures, like employer sanctions or tamper-proof identity cards, on immigration issues, but its main thrust is to reduce or eliminate the influx of immigrants. It proposes a moratorium on all immigrant entries, except that of spouses and minor children of United States citizens, "and legitimate refugees fleeing political persecution." Describing this immigration cutback as "a short pause," FAIR nonetheless says its moratorium would last as long as it takes to achieve the following goals:

1) Substantially eliminate illegal immigration; 2) implement an improved set of documents and procedures to verify work eligibility; 3) revise immigration laws to cut overall numbers; 4) complete "a comprehensive analysis of the long-term demographic, environmental resource, urban resource, cultural and employment/economic affects [sic] of future immigration and population growth."[11]

In southern California, an Orange County grand jury endorsed a three-year immigration moratorium as a way to ease demand on public services. The jury's report linked all immigration, but primarily illegal immigrants, with over-crowding of schools, jails, and housing, the spread of diseases, and the county's failure to win the drug war. The *Los Angeles Times* immediately found the proposal "unrealistic" and "unfortunate."

"The Hispanic community is outraged," declared Alfredo Amezcua, past president of the Hispanic Bar Association of

Orange County.[12] "It appears that the only thing immigrants are not to blame for is earthquakes."

Border Control and Other Issues

FAIR's last goal indicates how sketchy present knowledge is of the real effects of immigrants, legal or illegal, on many aspects of society and the economy. On that point most sides agree. Agreement is also found on the nation's need to appear in control of its borders.

Former President Ronald Reagan once said, "This country has lost control of its own borders, and no country can sustain that kind of position." It's a refrain repeated by President Clinton and many others across the political spectrum. Even pro-immigrant groups, like the National Forum, and ethnic advocates, such as the National Council for La Raza, admit that stopping illegal immigrants at the borders is of increasing importance. They add that this must be done in humane ways that respect people's civil rights, entailing better oversight and training of border agents.

Because of the problem's very nature, no one can know how big it really is, how much it changes from year to year, or exactly how the illegal population affects different aspects of society and the economy. The supposed impacts, as sketched in the previous chapters, heavily influence the current debate. In the name of heading off stronger measures, some lawmakers have called for boosting the strength of the Border Patrol, adding military forces to bolster border control efforts, and charging border-crossers a fee to finance the heightened measures.

Immigrant proponents, such as California lawmaker and Latino caucus chair Richard G. Polanco, agree with some of these steps but argue that enforcing labor laws and employer sanctions would be more effective in discouraging the illegals.

Governor Wilson, who believes illegal immigrants are drawn to California by social services, urges tougher steps against them. He wants to withhold citizenship to children born in America if their parents are in the country illegally. This would require amending the U.S. Constitution. Governor Wilson would also bar illegals' children from schools and withhold from their families all but emergency health care. His opponents call these proposals "barbaric," but politicians in other impacted states are weighing the pros and cons of supporting similar measures.

One thing is certain: Legal residents, who have gone through the obstacle course, feel that illegals cheat them. These immigrants object to illegals being allowed to cut in line, as it were, for any of the benefits of living and working in the United States. In the end, a rising sense of injustice may combine with baser motives to impose harsher measures than the real problems require. If so, American history suggests that innocents will suffer and citizens will later come to regret the excesses they once approved.

It is time to invest in gathering facts and fashioning an unbiased analysis of the contributions and impacts of immigrants—both legal and illegal. Do they help or harm the economy, and in what ways? Is their tax support of health and welfare services outweighed by their use of those services?

How far should we go to help children and adults, who have other languages and cultures, gain education and skills? Are immigrants more likely than natives to be involved in crime, and if so, as predator or prey?

Fears of social change and fragmentation inflame the issues embodied by such questions. Perhaps, along with facts and analysis, we need to probe our own values and hopes, define our personal vision of what America is all about. There is no better moment to wrestle with inescapable change than now.

Notes by Chapter

Chapter 1

1. Pamela Lopez-Johnson, "New U.S. Citizen Is Celebrating a Special Fourth," *Santa Barbara News-Press,* July 4, 1993, p. B1.

2. Seth Mydans, "Refugee Has Rare Chance to Be in 'Heaven'," *New York Times,* August 22, 1993, p. 1.

3. Eugene Robinson, "Worldwide Migration Nears Crisis: Politics, Economics Cited in U.N. Study," *The Washington Post,* July 7, 1993, p. A1.

4. U.S. Immigration and Naturalization Service, *Statistical Yearbook of the Immigration and Naturalization Service, 1991* (Washington, D.C.: U.S. Government Printing Office, 1992), p. 27.

5. Tom Morganthau, "America: Still a Melting Pot?" *Newsweek,* August 9, 1993, pp. 18–19.

6. Dianne Klein, "Majority in State Are Fed Up With Illegal Immigration," *Los Angeles Times,* September 19, 1993, p. A1.

7. *1991 INS Yearbook,* p. 37.

8. Ibid., p. 18.

9. U.S. Immigration and Naturalization Service, *Statistical Yearbook of the Immigration and Naturalization Service, 1990* (Washington, D.C.: U.S. Government Printing Office, 1991), pp. 31–32.

10. *1991 INS Yearbook,* p. 21.

11. Ibid., Table B, p. 19.

12. Ibid., p. 23.

13. Ibid., Table 17, p. 61.

14. Quoted in "Southern California Voices: A Forum for Community Issues," *Los Angeles Times,* August 9, 1993, p. B5.

15. Joel Kotkin, "Whatever Happened to the Ideal of Citizenship?" *Los Angeles Times,* July 11, 1993, p. M1.

16. Chris Kraul and Jennifer Warren, "Last Chinese Emigrants Fly Home," *Los Angeles Times,* July 20, 1993, p. A3.

17. U.S. National Research Council, Panel on Immigration Statistics, *Immigration Statistics: A Story of Neglect* (Washington, D.C.: National Academy Press, 1985), p. 2.

18. "What Is the Federation for American Immigration Reform?," a fact sheet published by FAIR.

19. "Immigration and Naturalization Service's General Operations and Fiscal Year 1993 Budget," hearing before the Subcommittee on International Law, Immigration and Refugees of the Judiciary Committee, House of Representatives, March 25, 1992, Washington, D.C., pp. 160–165.

20. "Why We Want Your Help in Fighting Nativism," undated backgrounder by Frank Sharry, National Immigration Forum, p. 3.

21. NBC News Special, The Brokaw Report: "Immigration, the Good, the Bad, the Illegal," March 27, 1993.

22. Ibid.

Chapter 2

1. John F. Kennedy *A Nation of Immigrants* (New York: Harper & Row, Publishers, 1964), pp. 13–14.

2. Ibid., p. 9.

3. Yuji Ichioka, *The Issei: The World of the First Generation Japanese Immigrants, 1885–1924*, (New York: Macmillan, Inc., 1988), p. 1

4. Eric Forner and John A. Garraty, eds., *The Reader's Companion to American History* (Boston: Houghton Miffin Co., 1991), p. 27.

5. Benjamin Franklin, "The German Language in Pennsylvania," cited by James Crawford, ed., in *Language Loyalties: A Source Book on the Official English Controversy* (Chicago: University of Chicago Press, 1992), p. 18.

6. U.S. Immigration and Naturalization Service, *Statistical Yearbook of the Immigration and Naturalization Service, 1990* (Washington, D.C.: U.S. Government Printing Office, 1992), pp. 13, 47.

7. Oscar Handlin, *A Pictorial History of Immigration* (New York: Crown Publishing Group, 1972), p. 101.

8. Forner and Garraty, p. 780.

9. Kennedy, p. 71.

10. *1990 INS Yearbook*, p. 15.

11. Calvin D. Linton, ed., *The Bicentennial Almanac: 200 Years of America* (Nashville, Tenn.: Thomas Nelson, Inc., 1975), p. 196.

12. *1990 INS Yearbook,* pp. 17–18.

13. Barbara Benton, *Ellis Island: A Pictorial History* (New York: Facts on File Publications, 1985), p. 34.

14. Ibid.

15. Ichioka, pp. 40, 52.

16. Ibid., p. 212.

17. Richard Drinnon, *Keeper of Concentration Camps: Dillion S. Meyer and American Racism* (Berkeley, Calif.: University of California Press, 1987), p. 8.

18. *1992 Congressional Quarterly Almanac* (Washington, D.C.: Congressional Quarterly Inc., 1992), pp. 335–336.

19. Benton, p. 34.

20. Leon F. Bouvier and Robert W. Gardner, "Immigration to the U.S.: The Unfinished Story," *Population Bulletin*, November 1986, p. 9.

21. U.S. Immigration and Naturalization Service, *An Immigrant Nation: United States Regulation of Immigration, 1798–1991* (Washington, D.C.: U.S. Government Printing Office, 1991), p. 14.

22. U.S. Immigration and Naturalization Service, *Statistical Yearbook of the Immigration and Naturalization Service, 1991* (Washington, D.C.: U.S. Government Printing Office, 1992), p. 27.

23. *Bicentennial Almanac*, pp. 236–237.

24. *1990 INS Yearbook*, p. 20.

25. Wilton S. Tifft, *Ellis Island* (Chicago: Contemporary Books, 1990), p. 75.

26. Benton, pp. 92–96.

27. *1990 INS Yearbook*, p. 25.

28. *1991 INS Yearbook*, pp. 70, 84.

Chapter 3

1. Eric Forner and John A. Garraty, eds., *The Reader's Companion to American History*, (Boston: Houghton Miffin Co., 1991), p. 991.

2. U.S. Immigration and Naturalization Service, *Statistical Yearbook of the Immigration and Naturalization Service, 1991* (Washington, D.C.: U.S. Government Printing Office, 1992), p. 19.

3. "Provisions of 1990 Immigration Act," *Congressional Quarterly Almanac, 1990* (Washington, D.C.: Congressional Quarterly Inc., 1990), pp. 482–484.

4. U.S. Immigration and Naturalization Service, *An Immigrant Nation: United States Regulation of Immigration, 1798–1991* (Washington, D.C.: U.S. Government Printing Office, 1991), p. 32.

5. *1991 INS Yearbook*, pp. 15–21.

6. Martha Farnsworth Riche, "We're All Minorities Now," *American Demographics*, October 1991, p. 28.

7. *1991 INS Yearbook*, pp. 114–116.

8. Ibid., p. 117.

9. Ibid., p. 77.

10. Michael Fix and Wendy Zimmermann, "Immigrant Policy in the States: A Wavering Welcome" (Washington, D.C.: The Urban Institute, 1993), p. 20.

11. Raju Cheblum, "Last of Haitians Escape 'HIV Prison' in Cuba," *Santa Barbara News-Press,* June 22, 1993, p. A3.

12. Patrick J. McDonell and William J. Eaton, "Political Asylum System Under Fire, Faces Revision," *Los Angeles Times,* July 19, 1993, p. A1.

13. Ibid., p. 92.

14. U.S. Department of Justice, Immigration and Naturalization Service, *Immigration Reform and Control Act: Report on the Legalized Alien Population* (Washington, D.C.: U.S. Government Printing Office, 1992), p. *viii.*

15. *1991 INS Yearbook,* p. 95.

Chapter 4

1. Deborah Sontag, "Unlicensed Peddlers, Unfettered Dreams," *New York Times,* June 14, 1993, p. A1.

2. NBC News Special, The Brokaw Report: "Immigration, the Good, the Bad, the Illegal," March 27, 1993.

3. Michael J. Mandel and Christopher Farrell, "The Immigrants: How They're Helping to Revitalize the U.S. Economy," *Business Week,* July 13, 1992, p. 118.

4. Patrick Lee, "Studies Challenge View That Immigrants Harm Economy," *Los Angeles Times,* August 13, 1993, p. A1.

5. "Immigration Is a Labor Issue," Federation for American Immigration Reform, issue brief, March 22, 1993.

6. Rick Gladstone, "The Economics of Immigration," *San Francisco Chronicle,* June 13, 1993, p. E3.

7. "Immigration Overview," 1992 fact sheet from the Federation for American Immigration Reform.

8. Sonia Nazaro, "For This Union, It's War," *Los Angeles Times,* August 19, 1993, p. A1.

9. Lawrence E. Harrison, "America and Its Immigrants," *The National Interest,* Summer 1992, p. 39.

10. George J. Borjas and Richard B. Freeman, eds., *Immigration and the Work Force: Economic Consequences for the United States and Source Areas* (Chicago: The University of Chicago Press, 1992), p. 1.

11. Josh Getlin, "Crusader of the Cane," *Los Angeles Times,* February 7, 1993, p. E1.

12. Thomas Muller, *Immigrants and the American City* (New York: New York University Press, 1993), pp. 142–143.

13. "The Impact of Immigrants on the U.S.: Shattering the Myths," undated position paper, National Immigration Forum.

14. Tom Morganthau, "America: Still a Melting Pot?" *Newsweek,* August 9, 1993, pp. 18–19.

15. Lee, p. A1.

16. Willian B. Johnston and Arnold H. Packer, *Workforce 2000: Work and Workers for the 21st Century* (Indianapolis: The Hudson Institute, 1987), p. 96.

17. National Forum paper.

18. Mandel and Farrell, p. 116.

19. George J. Borjas, *Friends or Strangers: The Impact of Immigrants on the U.S. Economy* (New York: Basic Books, Inc., 1990), pp. 117, 219.

20. *1991 INS Yearbook,* pp. 143–144.

21. U.S. Department of Justice, Immigration and Naturalization Service, *Immigration Reform and Control Act: Report on the Legalized Alien Population* (Washington, D.C.: U.S. Government Printing Office, 1992), p. *viii.*

22. Ibid., p. 35.

23. *1991 INS Yearbook,* pp. 70–71.

Chapter 5

1. George J. Borjas, *Friends or Strangers: The Impact of Immigrants on the U.S. Economy* (New York: Basic Books, Inc., 1990), p. 159.

2. Federation for American Immigration Reform, undated paper, "U.S. Pays for Out-of-Control Immigration."

3. Richard D. Lamm and Gary Imhoff, *The Immigration Time Bomb: The Fragmenting of America* (New York: E. P. Dutton, 1985), pp. 159–161.

4. Patrick Lee, "Studies Challenge View That Immigrants Harm Economy," *Los Angeles Times,* August 13, 1993, p. A1. Also see Urban Institute review in Greg Miller, "Immigrant Costs Overstated, Study Finds," *Los Angeles Times,* September 3, 1993, p. B1.

5. Ibid., Miller.

6. National Immigration Forum, undated position paper, "The Impact of Immigrants on the U.S.: Shattering the Myths," pp. 2–3.

7. Alan C. Miller and Ronald J. Ostrow, "Immigration Policy Failures Invite Overhaul," *Los Angeles Times,* July 11, 1993, A1.

8. "Immigrant Schools: The Wrong Lessons," *Newsweek,* August 9, 1993, p. 23.

9. Glenn F. Bunting, "Wilson's Huge Bill to U.S. Uses Sleight of Hand," *Los Angeles Times,* February 8, 1993, p. A3.

10. Michael Fix and Wendy Zimmermann, "Immigrant Policy in the States: A Wavering Welcome," a report, Washington, D.C.: The Urban Institute, 1993, pp. 1–2.

11. Ibid., pp. 20–21.

12. Irene Wielawski, "Health Systems in Bind on Care for Illegal Immigrants," *Los Angeles Times,* August 31, 1993, p. A1.

13. U.S. Department of Justice, Immigration and Naturalization Service, *Immigration Reform and Control Act: Report on the Legalized Alien Population* (Washington, D.C.: U.S. Government Printing Office, 1992), p. 47.

14. Ibid., p. 51.

15. Barbara Benton, *Ellis Island: A Pictorial History* (New York: Facts On File Publications, 1985), pp. 25–31.

Chapter 6

1. Karen Felzer, "Could My Friend Really Be an Immigrant?" *Los Angeles Times,* February 8, 1993, p. B4.

2. Katsuyo K. Howard, ed., *Passages: An Anthology of the Southeast Asian Refugee Experience* (Fresno, Calif.: California State University, 1990), p. 139.

3. Lorraine M. McDonnell and Paul T. Hill, *Newcomers in American Schools: Meeting the Educational Needs of Immigrant Youth* (Santa Monica, Calif: RAND, 1993), p. 42.

4. Michael Fix and Wendy Zimmermann, "Educating Immigrant Children: Chapter 1 in the Changing City" (Washington, D.C.: The Urban Institute, 1993), p. 10.

5. National Immigration Law Center, "Legal Needs and Barriers: The Case for Funding Representation of Aliens," August 1992, p. 14.

6. Michael Fix and Wendy Zimmermann, "Immigrant Policy in the States: A Wavering Welcome," (Washington, D.C.: The Urban Institute, 1993), p. 33.

7. McDonnell and Hill, p. 4.

8. Richard Estrada, "Schools and Ethnic Tensions," *The Dallas Morning News,* September 20, 1991, p. A19.

9. Thomas J. Lueck, "Immigrant Enrollment Rises in New York City Schools," *New York Times,* April 16, 1993, p. B1.

10. "U.S. Pays for Out-of-Control Immigration," Federation for American Immigration Reform, undated paper.

11. From U.S.ENGLISH's 1988 fundraising brochure, quoted by James Crawford, ed., in *Language Loyalties: A Source Book on the Official English Controversy* (Chicago: University of Chicago Press, 1992), pp. 144–147.

12. Frank Sharry, "Why Immigrants Are Good for America," *The Orlando Sentinel,* September 22, 1991, p. G1.

13. William J. Eaton, "Latinos Found Deeply Attached to U.S.," *Los Angeles Times,* December 16, 1992, p. A5.

14. Quoted by Frank Sharry, "Backgrounder for Advocates: Why We Want Your Help in Fighting Nativism," from National Immigration Forum.

15. David Wallechinsky, "This Land of Ours," *Parade,* July 5, 1992, p. 4.

16. McDonnell and Hill, pp. 56–57.

17. Ibid., pp. 61–63, 83

18. George E. Pozzetta, ed., *Contemporary Immigration and American Society,* Vol. 20 (New York: Garland Publishing, 1991), p. ix.

Chapter 7

1. Joseph C. Spencer, Jr., untitled anecdote in "Life in These United States," *Reader's Digest,* July 1993, p. 73. Reprinted with permission. Copyright 1993 by the Reader's Digest Association, Inc.

2. Michael Fix and Wendy Zimmermann, "Educating Immigrant Children: Chapter 1 in the Changing City" (Washington, D.C.: The Urban Institute, 1993), Exhibit 3.

3. Tom Morganthau, "America: Still a Melting Pot?" *Newsweek,* August 9, 1993, pp. 19, 25.

4. Quoted by Wilton S. Tifft, *Ellis Island* (Chicago: Contemporary Books, Inc., 1990), p. 58.

5. Evelyn W. Hersey's 1934 conference paper, quoted in Stanley Feldstein and Lawrence Costello, eds., *The Ordeal of Assimilation: A Documentary History of the White Working Class* (Garden City, N.Y.: Anchor Books, 1974), p. 399.

6. Robert Reinhold, "A Welcome for Immigrants Turns to Resentment," *New York Times,* August 25, 1993, p. A1.

7. Fernando de la Peña, *Democracy or Babel? The Case for Official English in the United States* (Washington, D.C.: U.S.ENGLISH, 1991), p. 40.

8. Peter Brimelow, "Time to Rethink Immigration?" *National Review,* June 22, 1992, pp. 44–45.

9. George F. Will, "Assimilation Is Not a Dirty Word," *Los Angeles Times,* July 29, 1993, p. B7.

10. *1991 INS Yearbook,* Table 41, p. 122.

11. Tad Szulc, "The Greatest Danger We Face," *Parade Magazine,* July 25, 1993, p. 4.

12. Julie Lee, "I Am You From Far Away," *Los Angeles Times,* April 5, 1993, p. B4. Excerpt used by permission of author; see newspaper for poem.

Chapter 8

1. John Aloysius Farrell, "Open Doors, Closing Minds," *Boston Globe,* February 23, 1992, p. 61.

2. Warren R. Leiden's May 6, 1992, letter to the editor in the *Christian Science Monitor.*

3. Otis L. Graham, Jr. and Roy Beck, "To Help Inner City, Cut Flow of Immigrants," *Los Angeles Times,* May 19, 1992, p. A11.

4. "FAIR's Recommendations on Asylum Reform," March 18, 1993.

5. Harold M. Launer and Joseph E. Palenski, eds., *Crime and the New Immigrants* (Springfield, Ill.: Charles C. Thomas, Publisher, 1989), p. *xiii.*

6. Quoted by Wilton S. Tifft, *Ellis Island* (Chicago: Contemporary Books, Inc., 1990), p. 58.

7. Tom Morganthau, "America: Still a Melting Pot?" *Newsweek,* August 9, 1993, p. 20.

8. Palmer Stacy and Wayne Lutton, *The Immigration Time Bomb,* rev. ed., (Monterey, Va.: The American Immigration Control Foundation, 1988), p. 101.

9. George James, "Crime Down in New York for 2d Year in Row," *New York Times,* March 19, 1993, P. A1. Also see Deborah Sontag, "A City of Immigrants Is Pictured in Report," *New York Times,* July 1, 1992, p. B1.

10. Stacy and Lutton, p. 105.

11. Thomas Muller, *Immigrants and the American City* (New York: New York University Press, 1993), p. 214.

12. Bernard Gavzer,"Held Without Hope," *Parade Magazine,* March 21, 1993, p. 4.

13.Stacy and Lutton, 1988, p. 108.

14. U.S. Department of Justice, *1992 Annual Report of the Attorney General of the United States* (Washington, D.C.: U.S. Government Printing Office, 1992), pp. 21–22.

15. *1991 INS Yearbook,* p. 146.

16. Deborah Sontag, "Study Sees Illegal Aliens in New Light," *New York Times,* September 2, 1993, p. B1.

17. Ibid., p. B8.

18. Milton D. Morris and Albert Mayio, *Curbing Illegal Immigration* (Washington, D.C.: The Brookings Institution, 1982), pp. 2–3.

19. U.S. Department of Justice, Immigration and Naturalization Service Statistics Division, *INS Fact Book: Summary of Recent Immigration Data,* July 1993, p. 24.

20. John Pomfret, "INS Criticized for Not Acting to Stem Smuggling of Asians by Gangs," *The Washington Post,* February 9, 1993, p. A4.

21. Deborah Sontag, "Immigrants Swindle Their Own, Preying on Trust," *New York Times,* August 25, 1992, p. B1.

Chapter 9

1. Oscar Handlin, *Statue of Liberty* (New York: Newsweek Book Division, 1971), p. 61.

2. Barbara Benton, *Ellis Island: A Pictorial History* (New York: Facts on File, Inc., 1985), p. 176.

3. Wilton S. Tifft, *Ellis Island* (Chicago: Contemporary Books, Inc., 1990), p. 205.

4. Federation for American Immigration Reform, fact sheet, "Summary of Key Findings: 1992 National Roper Poll on Immigration," 1992.

5. Lindsey Grant, ed., *Elephants in the Volkswagon: Facing the Tough Questions About Our Overcrowded Country* (New York: W. H. Freeman & Co., 1992), p. 168.

6. Palmer Stacy and Wayne Lutton, *The Immigration Time Bomb,* rev. ed., (Monterey, Va.: American Immigration Control Foundation, 1988), p. *viii.*

7. A statement in the National Forum's newspak of September 1, 1992.

8. George J. Borjas and Richard B. Freeman, eds., *Immigration and the Work Force: Economic Consequences for the United States and Source Areas* (Chicago: University of Chicago Press, 1992), p. 10.

9. Mark Schapiro, "Browns and Greens: Europe's New Eco-Fascists," *The Amicus Journal,* Winter 1992, p. 7.

10. Federation for American Immigration Reform issue brief, "America Needs a Moratorium on Immigration," March 1993.

11. Ibid.

12. Kevin Johnson, "Latinos Blast Grand Jury Call for Immigration Ban," *Los Angeles Times,* June 23, 1993, p. A18.

Glossary

alien—Any person not a citizen or national of the United States.

amnesty—A temporary program pardoning illegal immigrants (also known as legalized aliens) for unlawful entry, which lets them remain in the United States.

asylee—A person in the United States who had been granted asylum (see below).

asylum—Permission to remain in the United States granted to aliens who claim their safety is threatened in their own country because of their political or religious beliefs.

emigrant, émigré—A person who leaves his or her own country to live permanently in another country.

green card—The card (once green, now actually pink and white) that designates an immigrant to the United States as a permanent resident.

immigrant—A person who comes into a country to live there.

naturalization—The process by which an immigrant becomes a citizen.

permanent resident alien—A person legally entitled to live and work in the United States, a status usually achieved after an immigrant has lived in this country for three to five years.

quota—A numerical limit on immigrants allowed into the United States from another country.

refugee—Any person who fears persecution in his or her own country because of political or religious beliefs or has been forced to flee in wartime, and requests permission to enter the United States.

sponsor—A person or organization who accepts responsibility that an immigrant or refugee will have a place to live and will not require public assistance for at least three years.

visa—A permit allowing a foreigner to enter another country.

Further Reading

Benton, Barbara. *Ellis Island: A Pictorial History.* New York: Facts on File Publications, 1985.

Bogen, Elizabeth. *Immigration in New York.* New York: Praeger Publishers, 1987.

Borjas, George J., and Richard B. Freeman, eds. *Immigration and the Work Force: Economic Consequences for the United States and Source Areas.* Chicago: University of Chicago Press, 1992.

Crawford, James, ed. *Language Loyalties: A Source Book on the Official English Controversy.* Chicago: University of Chicago Press, 1992.

De la Peña, Fernando. *Democracy or Babel: The Case for Official English.* Washington, D.C.: U.S.ENGLISH, 1991.

Drinnon, Richard. *Keeper of Concentration Camps: Dillion S. Meyer and American Racism.* Berkeley, Calif.: University of California Press, 1987.

Dudley, William, ed. *Immigration: Opposing Viewpoints.* San Diego, Calif.: Greenhaven Press, 1990.

Ehrlich, Paul R., et al. *The Golden Door: International Migration, Mexico, and the United States.* New York: Ballantine Books, 1979.

Feldstein, Stanley, and Lawrence Costello, eds. *The Ordeal of Assimilation: A Documentary History of the White Working Class.* Garden City, N.Y.: Anchor Books, 1974.

Fix, Michael, et al. *Immigration and Immigrants: Setting the Record Straight.* Washington, D.C.: The Urban Institute, 1994.

Grant, Lindsey, ed. *Elephants in the Volkswagen: Facing the Tough Questions About Our Overcrowded Country.* New York: W. H. Freeman & Co., 1992.

Handlin, Oscar. *A Pictorial History of Immigration.* New York: Crown Publishers, 1972.

Hauser, Pierre, N. *Illegal Aliens.* New York: Chelsea House Publishers, 1990.

Howard, Katsuyo K., ed. *Passages: An Anthology of the Southeast Asian Refugee Experience.* Fresno, Calif.: California State University, 1990.

Ichioka, Yuji. *The Issei: The World of the First Generation Japanese Immigrants, 1885–1924.* New York: Macmillan, Inc., 1988.

Johnston, Willian B., and Arnold H. Packer. *Workforce 2000: Work and Workers for the 2lst Century.* Indianapolis: The Hudson Institute, 1987.

Juffras, Jason. *Impact of the Immigration Reform and Control Act on the Immigration and Naturalization Service.* Santa Monica, Calif.: RAND and The Urban Institute Press, 1991.

Kennedy, John F. *A Nation of Immigrants.* New York: Harper & Row, Publishers, 1964.

Lacey, Dan. *The Essential Immigrant.* New York: Hippocrene Books, 1990.

Lamm, Richard D., and Gary Imhoff. *The Immigration Time Bomb: The Fragmenting of America.* New York: E. P. Dutton, 1985.

Launer, Harold M., and Joseph E. Palenski. *Crime and the New Immigrants.* Springfield, Ill.: Charles Thomas, Publisher, 1989.

Levine, Daniel B., et al., eds. *Immigration Statistics: A Story of Neglect.* Washington, D.C.: National Academy Press, 1985.

Lewis, Sasha G. *Slave Trade Today: American Exploitation of Illegal Aliens.* Boston: Beacon Press, 1979.

Linton, Calvin D., ed. *The Bicentennial Almanac: 200 Years of America.* Nashville, Tenn.: Thomas Nelson, Inc. Publishers, 1975.

McDonnell, Lorraine M., and Paul T. Hill. *Newcomers in American Schools: Meeting the Educational Needs of Immigrant Youth.* Santa Monica, Calif.: RAND, 1993.

Muller, Thomas. *Immigrants and the American City.* New York: New York University Press, 1993.

Pozzetta, George E., ed. *Contemporary Immigration and American Society,* Vol. 20. New York: Garland Publishing, 1991.

Rieff, David. *Los Angeles: Capital of the Third World.* New York: Simon & Schuster, 1991.

Santoli, Al. *New Americans: Immigrants and Refugees in the U.S. Today (An Oral History).* New York: Viking Penguin, Inc., 1988.

Stacy, Palmer, and Wayne Lutton. *The Immigration Time Bomb,* rev. ed. Monterey, Va.: The American Immigration Control Foundation, 1988.

Tifft, Wilton S. *Ellis Island.* Chicago: Contemporary Books, Inc., 1990.

Index